So this w

Funny how ~~~~~~. No, the interloper who refused to return Granny Nell's home to its rightful owner had always resembled more of a shrew than someone's sweetheart.

"Buck up, Marine," he said on the release of a long breath. A bead of sweat trickled down his temple, and he ignored it. "Just another mission. Sometimes the enemy surprises you."

The girl in red met his gaze and stared a moment too long for his liking. Another five minutes in the car and he'd be toast.

Either he had to confront the enemy head on, or he had to retreat. Given the fact he wanted—no, *needed*—to have this situation under control, he chose the former.

Throwing the car door open, he stepped out onto the uneven sidewalk. In his estimation, a direct approach would get the job done.

Tossing his hat and shades on the seat, he let the door slam and palmed the keys. "Sophie Comeaux?"

Four sets of eyes swung their attention in his direction. "Yes, I'm Sophie," their leader said as she rose. "Who wants to know?"

Great. Now what?

He waited for a blue sedan to pass, then sprinted across the street to thrust his hand in her direction. "Ezra," he said. "Ezra Landry."

KATHLEEN MILLER is a tenth-generation Texan and mother of three grown sons and a teenage daughter. She is a graduate of Texas A&M University and an award-winning novelist of Christian and young-adult fiction. Kathleen is a former treasurer for the American Christian Fiction Writers and is a member of Inspirational Writers Alive, Words for the Journey, and The Authors Guild. Find out more about Kathleen at www.kathleenybarbo.com

Books by Kathleen Miller

HEARTSONG PRESENTS
HP474—You Can't Buy Love
HP529—Major League Dad
HP571—Bayou Fever
HP659—Bayou Beginnings
HP675—Bayou Secrets
HP691—Bayou Dreams

The Dwelling Place

Kathleen Miller

Heartsong Presents

In honor of the Buckner Children's Home in Dallas, Texas, which sheltered my grandmother, Mary Catherine Bottoms Aycock, and taught her to love Jesus so she could sing "Jesus Loves Me" with authority to her grandchildren and great-grandchildren. To find out more about the Buckner Children's Home or to make a donation, go to their Web site at www.bucknerchildren.org

A note from the Author:
I love to hear from my readers! You may correspond with me by writing:

> **Kathleen Miller**
> **Author Relations**
> **PO Box 721**
> **Uhrichsville, OH 44683**

ISBN 1-59789-055-3

THE DWELLING PLACE

Our mission is to publish and distribute inspirational products offering exceptional value and biblical encouragement to the masses.

PRINTED IN THE U.S.A.

one

June 14—Lake Charles, Louisiana

"A pity her mama couldn't be here to see this day," Great-Aunt Alta said.

Sophie Comeaux smiled at her only living relative and held her wedding bouquet a bit closer to her chest. Although she walked down the long aisle to the altar alone tonight, the presence of Mama and Daddy enveloped her.

She wore Mama's dress, cut down and hemmed to fit by one of the other marine wives, and a veil borrowed from the company commander's sister. Tied with a white ribbon among the flowers in her bouquet was the porcelain rosebud Daddy gave her when she was accepted to nursing school at Tulane.

"And they chose to marry on Flag Day. Isn't it wonderful? I'm sure Jim won't ever forget his anniversary." This from a distant cousin of her future husband's seated on the Hebert side of the chapel.

Mrs. James Wilson Hebert III.

Sophie Comeaux-Hebert.

Sophie Hebert.

The last one suited her best. Simple and uncomplicated like the life she and Jim would have. No matter where the Marine Corps sent her husband, like the Proverbs 31 woman she would be at his side doing her part.

Through the white haze of her veil, she saw Jim and his groomsmen exchange glances, then look down the aisle toward her. At the sight of her groom, her heart did a flip-flop. No handsomer man ever wore the uniform of the United States Marine Corps.

Her shoes began to pinch, and still she continued her slow

and dignified pace. The white pumps had been chosen for looks and not long-distance walking. Unless Jim disapproved, however, she'd kick them off once they got to the reception.

"I can't believe she gave up her job for him."

Sophie glanced to her left and saw her coworkers sitting together. Julie, Pam, Lydia, and Noreen waved while Dr. Campbell merely nodded. The new girl who had taken her place, Crystal, smiled. In return she winked.

She'd go back once Jim's career settled down. A marine on the way up needed the flexibility to move when the call came.

Closer now to the altar and she could see her future in-laws turning to stare. She got along well enough with Jim's dad, but his mother. . .well, that relationship would have to grow over time.

Sophie focused on Jim now, moving toward him like a ship following a beacon. Indeed, that's how it felt to be in Jim's world. First Lieutenant Hebert was a force of nature, a man who excelled in anything he attempted.

She met his gaze and smiled, her fingers tightening around the bouquet of white roses and pink ribbons. Behind Jim on the rail, a fat white candle burned in memory of her parents and Jim's grandmother, all three gone home to Jesus in the last year.

Look, Mama and Daddy. Your little girl is getting married.

"You look lovely," the pastor whispered as he met her on the steps.

To her right, two of the wives from Jim's outfit wore matching pink dresses while the maid of honor, Jim's best friend's sister, wore dark fuchsia. She offered the three of them a smile. Though she barely knew them now, no doubt they would soon be fast friends.

Sophie turned her head slightly so she could see Jim. In his dress uniform with sword and scabbard at his hip, he looked like a prince ready to carry her off for a happily-ever-after life.

No, she wouldn't miss school or work or anything about her old life. From this day forward, she would cleave to her husband and become one.

With Jim as her husband, she needed nothing or no one else.

Close enough to smell Jim's aftershave, Sophie inhaled deeply. She looked into the depths of his brown eyes and saw, what? Concern, that was it. Worry that her shoes were pinching. Of course, Jim was thoughtful that way.

"It'll be fine," she whispered.

Jim grasped her hand and looked away. Had the pastor said something while she'd been focused on Jim? Probably.

He squeezed her hand, and she thought of the promise he'd made last night after the rehearsal dinner. "You and I could make beautiful babies together, Sophie. Many beautiful babies."

Babies. Her heart did a flip-flop. Oh yes, she wanted many beautiful babies.

Until she met Jim, her babies had been the ones in the nursery at Charity Hospital where she volunteered on weekends. Now, with a ring and a promise, she would have babies all her own. And that new life began today. Now. Here.

I will remember every moment of this day forever.

"Sophie, are you listening?"

She blinked hard and looked up to see the reverend staring at her. On her right, the bridesmaids were snickering while, on her left, Jim looked positively disgusted.

"Pay attention," Jim whispered.

Mouthing a quick "I'm sorry," Sophie handed her bouquet off to the woman Jim had selected as matron of honor and took Jim's hands. They were cold. Or maybe she was just flushed from all the excitement.

"Wait!"

The pastor set his Bible down and leaned over the podium to stare at Jim. "Did you say something, son?"

Jim squeezed her hands, then released them. "I'm sorry, Sophie." He stared past her for a minute, then turned to look into the congregation. "There won't be a wedding today. I can't do this."

After that, things began to move in slow motion. To her right, the maid of honor dropped the bouquet, and the rose splintered at Sophie's feet.

And so did Sophie's heart.

❧

Veterans Hospital, New Orleans

"It's me, Dad. Ezra. It's Flag Day. I thought you might want a flag for your bed."

Robert Boudreaux barely spared Ezra a glance, choosing to grunt in agreement to the statement. Ezra went about the business of tying the small flag to the metal bed, all the while trying to think of what Jesus would do in this circumstance.

But then Joseph the carpenter would never have ended up in Veterans Hospital looking twice his age and sporting a rap sheet that included burglary, petty theft, and the desertion of at least one wife and son, and probably more. And those were only the transgressions Ezra was aware of.

Who knew how many more women like his mother had firsthand knowledge of this man's wandering ways? For all he knew, he could have brothers and sisters all over Louisiana.

Ezra checked the diagnosis on the label affixed to the bed. The old man was in sick bay for boozing again. Like as not he'd die of kidney failure or bad judgment before he hit sixty, if one of the women from his checkered past didn't kill him first.

Only through the Lord's good graces had Ezra's mother escaped the knowledge of who her husband really was. No, until Mama took sick, Dad kept his wild ways a secret. Either that or he walked a straight path for her. Ezra liked to think it was the latter.

After she died, Dad ran off. But then Dad's way of handling things was to run. Always had been.

Lord, don't let me be like him.

"What you wearing there?"

Ezra straightened his spine and forced himself to stare into the eyes of the man who had abandoned him. "A Marine Corps uniform, sir."

His father chuckled. "You, a marine? I hardly think so. You were born bayou trash, and you'll stay that way. Tell me another joke."

Fists clenched, Ezra called on all the faith he had to pray that God would intervene and turn this sour old man sweet again. "I'm a Green Beret, Dad. I just made major, and General Scanlon says I'm the kind of soldier he's looking for to head up some highly classified special operations out of—"

"There you go lying to me again." He reached for the rail and shifted up far enough to press the button and call a nurse. "Hey, this kid's bothering me. Thinks I'm his daddy. Come get rid of him. I ain't got no son, not one I want to spend time with, anyway."

"Buck up, Marine," Ezra said under his breath. "That's the booze talking. You have nothing to do with the demons chasing him."

"You talking to yourself, boy? Gone crazy in the head or something?"

A male nurse appeared at the door. "What's the problem, sir?"

His father fell back against the pillows. "Tell me what that man's name tag says."

"Ezra Landry," the nurse said. "So?"

"So he ain't my son, and I ain't having no visitors lessen it's my wife."

"I'm a Landry because he gave me up to his sister and brother-in-law to raise," he told the nurse. "You have a wife, Dad?" Ezra fixed his attention on the old man, even though he wanted nothing more than to look away from the emaciated mess his father had become. "Since when?"

"Since I say so," he replied. "And she's gonna come bail me out of this joint just as soon as she can."

The nurse gave Ezra a look that spoke volumes. Evidently Lieutenant Colonel Robert Boudreaux, Retired, was not the most popular patient at Veterans Hospital.

"Guess what?" his father asked the nurse. "He just made major. Big deal. Back in 'Nam we had the majors fetching our bullets for us."

"All right, I'm going," Ezra said. "You take care now. I'm shipping out a week from Thursday so I don't know when I'll see you again."

"Don't bother," his father said with a wave of his hand. "I travel light. Never did have any use for young'uns."

two

"Anybody home?" Sophie clutched the cassette tape of Sunday's sermon in one hand and knocked with the other. "Mrs. Landry? It's Sophie Comeaux from the church."

She stepped away from the door and checked the address on the card. 421B Riverside Avenue. Assuming the door on the left was A, this one would be B.

"All right, I'll try this one more time."

She pressed the bell and leaned against the door to be sure it rang. A split second after she heard the sound she was listening for, she heard another. It sounded like a thud followed by a weak cry.

"Mrs. Landry? Hello? Are you all right?"

Another muffled sound and Sophie decided someone inside was in trouble. She set the cassette on the porch rail and reached for the knob. The door swung open.

"Mrs. Landry?" She peered inside and found a woman of mature years sitting on a rug cradling her arm.

"Are you the sermon lady from church? Emmeline told me they'd be sending someone new."

Sophie knelt beside the woman and began to do a visual assessment. "Yes, ma'am, I'm new all right. Just moved to Latagnier last month. Figured if the Lord led me here He probably had work for me to do."

"Well, I like your gumption. Now I wonder if you might help me to the chair over there."

"Not yet, Mrs. Landry. Let me make sure you're not injured. Oh, I'm a nurse," she added.

She checked vitals as best she could while carrying on a

11

conversation with the talkative woman. Other than a possible fracture of her right wrist, she seemed fine.

"I'm going to need to call the ambulance," Sophie said. "They'll get that sore wrist patched up."

"Thank you, dear." She paused. "Do you work at the hospital here in Latagnier?"

"No, ma'am." Sophie rose. "I work for the state at the children's home."

She studied her injured wrist. "Do you now?"

"Yes, ma'am. I take care of the babies." Sophie made it all the way to the ancient black telephone in the hall before she stopped and went back. "Mrs. Landry, how about I drive you?"

"Oh, I would hate to trouble you. I'm sure you've got a husband and children waiting for you at home."

"No, ma'am, maybe someday but not today." She helped Mrs. Landry to stand. "Now let's get your purse and any medicines you're taking."

"Do you love children, Miss Comeaux, or are you just there for the paycheck?" Sophie's surprise must have shown. "Forgive an old woman her curiosity. I happen to have a soft spot in my heart for orphans. I was one for a time, you see, and until my husband passed on, the other side of this house was always filled with dear souls with no mama or daddy to care for them."

"Is that so?"

"How I do miss those days." Mrs. Landry smiled and placed her good hand atop Sophie's. "Well, before we go, could we pray first?"

☙

May 30, two years later

"My grandson's coming to see me, Sophie. I'm going to ask him to stay on permanently."

Sophie gulped down the heavily sweetened coffee along with what she longed to say and somehow managed a smile. Nell Landry tossed the words casually across the table, continuing to stir heavy cream into her Louisiana chicory-laden coffee as if she hadn't just uttered a statement that would change everything.

The woman had no children. How then could she have a grandchild? "Miss Nell, that's impossible."

Her friend's familiar broad grin emerged while she waved away the statement with a sweep of her blue-veined hand. "That's what you think," she said with a wink. "If I say I've got a grandson, then I do."

Sophie expelled a long breath. Of course. Nell had quite a reputation as a practical joker. The imaginary grandson surely had to be another prank. If she had a real grandson, he would most likely want to live in the other half of the duplex rather than with his grandmother in 421B.

She also would have mentioned him before now.

At least she hadn't made the move yet. There was still plenty of time to find another place for herself and the girls. Of course, with the adoption still pending, none of the homes she could afford would likely pass inspection.

Nell's place, with its cozy rooms and close proximity to the twins' school, had already garnered the approval of the caseworker. A change in the plans at this late date might jeopardize the entire process and possibly even send the precious five-year-olds back into the state's care.

Sophie shook her head and prayed away the thought. By the end of today's visit, the truth would prevail.

In the meantime, she decided to play along. "So tell me about this grandson of yours. Why haven't I met him?"

A shadow of something indefinable crossed her lined face. As quickly as it appeared, it was gone. "He's been away. In the military." She pushed aside the delicate porcelain cup and reached for the bundle Sophie had placed between them. "I know you have a. . .certain bias against that sort of fellow so I haven't mentioned him."

Rather than comment, she clutched the package to her chest. Only Nell knew about that time in her life. Well, Nell, the Lord, and a few hundred disappointed wedding guests back in Lake Charles.

"Enough of that now. I can see where your mind is headed, and I'm not going to let you go there. Not when there are so many other nice memories you could dwell on. Besides, you told me you gave that situation to the Lord. Isn't He big enough to handle your worries?"

"He is," Sophie said. "And I really am over it."

"If you were, honey, you wouldn't have to work so hard to try to convince me. Remember it's in His hands." Before Sophie could comment, Nell spoke again. "Let me see what you brought today. This looks too big to be this week's sermon tape."

Sophie relaxed and began to clear the table of the refreshments Nell insisted precede their twice-weekly visits. "Consider it an early birthday present. Do you like it?"

Only the soft hum of the window-unit air conditioner answered the question. Sophie settled the cups and plates on the immaculately clean kitchen counter and slipped back into the dining room to find the older woman staring at the book cradled in her hands.

"It's a Bible," Nell whispered. "The King James Version just like my old one." She paused. "Only this one has print big enough for me to read without my magnifying glass." Her smile went soft. "Oh, Sophie. . ."

"So you *do* like it?"

"Oh no, Sophie, I *love* it. Now I shall be able to read aloud again. With my other Bible, it was all I could do to hold the magnifying glass and understand the words, old woman that I am."

"You might have me bested in years, Miss Nell, but I would wager between the two of us, you're the younger in spirit." Sophie returned to her seat and shook her head. "I didn't know you preferred to read scripture aloud."

Nell cradled the Bible to her chest with one hand and reached across the table to touch Sophie's sleeve with the other. "Sweet child, if you only knew how many hours I spent at my grandmama's knee listening to her read the Good Book. There's nothing like hearing scripture spoken aloud, don't you agree?"

"Yes, I suppose."

"You suppose?" She set the Bible on the table and opened its cover. "Didn't anyone read you the Bible, Sophie?"

"No, ma'am."

"Oh, now there's a wrong I can right. Let me see here. . . ." Her words trailed off as she turned to the first page of the book of Genesis. "Here 'tis." Soon the majestic words of the Creator floated across the dining room in the slightly shaky voice of the dearest lady on earth.

Sophie let the words curl around her heart and sink deep inside. Never would she read Genesis without thinking of the verses being spoken in the genteel drawl of one of the last grand ladies of the South.

Sinking into the carved rosewood chair directly across from Nell, Sophie closed her eyes and let her memory tumble back in time to the day she arrived at Nell's doorstep. One more needy old lady to visit with a tape of the Sunday sermon and she'd have had her final good deed of the day checked off. She would have satisfied the Lord, earned her reward, and gone home to block out the worries of the world with a pint of ice cream and whatever was on television.

An awful way to look at serving the Lord, but back then that had been her version of good works. No wonder she'd been so miserable.

When Nell Landry had the bad luck to fall on her way to answer the doorbell that day, Sophie's nursing training took over. Nothing since that moment had been the same.

It was as if the Lord heard her cry and sent an elderly guardian angel just shy of earning her wings. That guardian angel, in turn, had pointed her in the right direction and given her the courage to adopt a pair of pint-sized angels in training. Every day she thanked Him for sending Nell Landry and the twins.

"Sophie, honey, you haven't heard a word I've said, have you?"

Her eyes opened to see Nell's smile had turned down a bit at the corners. "I'm sorry," she answered. "You caught me thinking."

Nell closed the Bible and rested her hand on the brown leather cover. "I was afraid of that. A penny for your thoughts?"

Stretching her arm across the table, she covered Sophie's hand with fingers still strong and agile despite nearly seventy-five years of use. Sophie tried in vain to suppress a smile. "I was thinking of the day you and I first met."

Nell nodded slowly. "Troublesome old woman, wasn't I?"

"Absolutely not."

"And you thought you were just doing a kind deed for the church." Nell patted her hand. "I'll wager a guess you never expected to spend the night in the emergency room holding one hand of an old fool while the other got bound in a cast." Her eyes, the color of strong-brewed coffee, barely blinked. "Ezra will like you."

Sophie glanced past the elderly woman to the broad expanse of hallway covered in brightly colored Persian rugs, the cause of her accident. She chose to ignore the subject of the imaginary grandson in favor of a more practical topic.

"I don't know why you don't roll up some of these rugs. They're a hazard, and you know it."

"They're my memories, and *you* know it. Now stop trying to steer me off track. I'm not that old." Her fingers tightened. "It won't change a thing when Ezra comes to stay here, you know," she said, quickly jumping from one subject to another.

Sophie, used to the lightning-fast changes in conversation, merely shrugged and waited for her to explain.

"In two weeks the carpenters come to finish the work next door." Nell withdrew her hand. "When they're done, you and the girls will be moving in, and that's final. Besides, you do want to finalize the adoption before Christmas, don't you?"

"Of course." Sophie sighed. "Miss Nell, if I ask you a question, will you promise to give me an honest answer, even if you think it might hurt me?"

Nell seemed to consider this a moment. "I promise, dear, and what have I told you about making a promise?"

"Never make one unless you're prepared to live up to what you promise."

She sat back and lifted the teacup. "That's right. Now what was it you wanted to ask?"

Taking a deep breath, Sophie let it out slowly. "I was wondering. Do you really think I will make a good mom for Chloe and Amanda?"

Her hostess set the cup down without taking a sip. "Sophie Comeaux, don't you ever wonder that. You were handpicked by the Lord and a meddlesome old woman to be mama to those girls. If He didn't want you to go through with it, how do you explain the fact that everything is falling into place so nicely?"

"I assumed that was because you're on a first-name basis with just about everyone at the orphans' home."

Nell winked. "Well now, I will admit I know one or two folks down there, but, dear, if this is meant to be, it will be the Lord who gets the credit."

"Maybe so, Miss Nell, but somehow I think the Lord might have enlisted you to do a bit of His work for Him."

three

"She is not moving in and living next door without paying rent or submitting to a background check. It's neither practical nor safe."

Major Ezra Landry managed a carefully practiced look that would crush the most fearless marine. Of course, it didn't faze Granny Nell.

"That's final," he added with an authority he knew he did not carry inside these walls. "Now let's get back to the Lord's Word."

Ezra peered at his adopted grandmother, his father's child-less elder sister, and frowned. This meeting hadn't gone nearly as he planned. While Granny Nell always welcomed him with open arms and never mentioned his extended absence, she'd sure given him a shock this time around when she told him her plans.

True, she had reached the age where she needed more care than a woman living alone could manage. True, also, she *did* have half a house sitting empty next door.

Still, did she have to take in a *total stranger*? Why, there was nothing but a paper-thin wall between the two dwellings, and who knew what sort of person might be on the other side? And if Nell weren't playing another one of her practical jokes, this person had just showed up on her doorstep one day with a sermon tape and a hard-luck story.

Okay, so he *imagined* she'd given Granny Nell a hard-luck story. It had to be true, though, for Nell held a soft spot in her heart for widows and orphans. Now that she was no longer up to the job of driving herself to volunteer at the orphanage in New Iberia, like as not she'd decided to go back to taking them in herself.

If only he'd been in a position to move in. Unfortunately, in his line of work, that was impossible.

"So when do I meet your friend? What was her name?"

"Sophie," she said. "Sophie Comeaux. And she's with her great-aunt this week. The dear woman just had surgery, and evidently Sophie's all she has left."

"Then let her stay there." Ezra held up his hand to quiet his grandmother's protest. "I'm sorry. I shouldn't have said that."

"The Word of the Lord says we should take in those in need and care for those who cannot care for themselves," Nell said, defiance written all over her gently worn features. "He also says He will take the widows and the childless and place them in homes with families." She thumped the brown leather volume in her lap. "Psalm 68, verses 5 and 6, of my King James Bible. Look it up for yourself. You do have your Bible with you, don't you, young man?"

No thanks, Granny Nell. I know that one by heart. "I'm nearly thirty. When are you going to stop calling me 'young man'?"

She peered up at him. "Long as I remember that I used to change your diapers and your daddy's, I suppose."

"Ever hear from my dad?"

"He's in jail again." She looked away, a tiredness etching her features. "This time up at Angola. I don't s'pose he'll come out alive this time."

The state prison—home to felons and hard cases. It figured. "Well, at least we know where to find him now. Not that anyone would want to do that."

Granny Nell swung her attention back to him. "Son, I know what you're up to, and it won't work."

Ezra had seen the look she gave him before, and he knew better than to continue with this kind of diversionary tactic. Instead he decided to guide the conversation to smoother waters.

"I've got pictures from some of the places I've been," he

said. "I left them in the car, but I can go get them. I brought a couple of new handkerchiefs, too."

She nodded, and peace was once again restored. For the next three days, the topic of the gold-digging woman from Latagnier Fellowship Church of Grace was ignored in favor of good conversation and even better home cooking.

Ezra feasted on cheese grits and biscuits at breakfast; fried catfish, cornbread, and black-eyed peas for lunch; and the most delicious Southern ham and redeye gravy for dinner with bread pudding for dessert. Leaving would be hard, and not just because he would miss the good food.

For all her advanced years, Nell Landry could still set a fine table. Of course he had the sneaking suspicion all the cooking, which she'd made him help with, had been designed to distract him from the unpleasant topic floating unspoken between them.

Instead of discussing what was really wrong, they reminisced about years gone by, laughed over Nell's latest practical jokes, and talked about the places he'd been. Once again he briefly entertained the thought that the story of the Comeaux woman moving in might be another of Nell's jokes, but he dared not ask.

Not as long as the company was good and the food even better. He'd be unfit for field command, however, if he stayed another day.

A few hours before departure time, Ezra pushed away from the table, leaving a few bites of the best bread pudding on earth still uneaten. His stomach full and the last evening of his stay nearly at a close, the time had come to broach the topic of Sophie Comeaux.

He took a deep breath and let it out slowly, folding the fancy white napkin with care as he asked the Lord to give him the words to convince Granny Nell of the error of her ways. Nothing definite came to him, so he struck out on his own.

"Will you listen to a little advice?" he began, knowing full well these were the words she had used with him more than once. "And realize I'm only saying this because I love you." Again words that had come from Granny Nell's mouth too many times to count.

She nodded. A good sign. Usually if Nell intended to put up a fight, she did it right away.

A more straightforward female had never lived, and for this Ezra adored her. No other woman had ever matched up to his grandmother's common sense, tough love, and decent Christian values. He trusted her opinions above all others and knew her judgment to be 100 percent correct on most matters.

This made the current situation even more worrisome.

Ezra squared his shoulders and began to fold the napkin in half. "Now I know you've told me this Sophie person was sent out here from the church, so in theory she can't be all bad. The Lord does look after His own." While his grandmother nodded, Ezra paused to choose his next words carefully. "And she *has* done a good job of keeping you company."

Nell opened her mouth to speak, then clamped her lips shut when he lifted his hand to stop her. Suitably chastised, she held her finger to her upper lip and smiled.

A good sign.

"Any woman willing to spend her days delivering sermon tapes and visiting with the elderly must have plenty of time on her hands. Doesn't she have a husband or a job? A family, maybe? What about this great-aunt of hers?"

Nell pursed her lips and seemed to be mulling over the questions. "Sophie is a good woman who should have had a husband and family a long time ago and would have if certain things hadn't happened." For a moment she seemed lost in thought. "She's a precious thing, just about your age," she said as she shook her head, "and not bigger than a minute. She's a nurse for the county and going to school part-time, too."

He nodded. "And?"

"And she has two precious girls, orphans both of them, like their mama, and—"

"I thought so." He slapped the top of his thigh with his free hand. "She's looking for a babysitter and a place to live. Tell me you didn't agree to this willingly."

Nell said nothing, but her soft brown eyes spoke volumes. Her backbone had gone stiff, most likely turned to solid steel.

Ezra blinked hard and tried to remember he only held the dear woman's best interests at heart. She'd pulled him out of more scrapes than he would ever remember and had stood by him in the biggest battles of his life.

Now it was his turn to take care of her.

"She didn't talk me into anything, young man," Nell said slowly, interrupting his thoughts. "In fact, it was me who had to do the convincing. That sweet young lady was almost at the end of her rope caring for those girls and trying to pay her rent when I offered to—"

Something snapped inside him. "When you offered to give her *my* house and *my* place in your life. You just let some woman from the church waltz in the door and talk you into adopting her like she was your own."

"You didn't seem to mind when I took you in," she said, her brown eyes blazing fire. "And who told you this was *your* house, Ezra Landry, even if you are my only living blood relative? The Lord provided this dwelling place when your grandfather took up preaching. Do you think it belongs to anyone but Him?"

She seemed to be waiting for an answer he couldn't give. He looked away and tried to control the insistent drumming in his temples.

"Ezra, this isn't about a house or even about who's right."

He gave her his attention but said nothing. Telling her she was wrong would only serve to bring an early end to the conversation. He knew this about Granny Nell, but then he always made it his business to know his opponent. In the field, it kept him alive; here in Granny Nell's house, it didn't seem to matter.

"Then what *is* it about, Granny?"

"It is about what's important to the Lord. Sophie, she believes she's got a corner on the guilt market. Now you—you're a man who believes the Lord has some kind of list up in heaven that He checks off when you're good and another He adds to when you mess up." She paused.

"Come to think of it, you two are very much alike. Neither one of you has completely grasped the full forgiveness that comes with the Lord's salvation."

"I never said that."

Her expression softened. "Nor do you deny it."

Blood pounded in his temples. Any other person would have drawn an immediate reaction. But this was Granny Nell.

"You're not listening to me," he managed to say through his clenched jaw. "I love you, and I want what is best for you." He made a grab for the ancient black telephone and held the receiver in his hand, thrusting it toward her. "You're just going to have to call and tell this woman you've changed your mind. She *does* have a phone, doesn't she?"

"I am not one of your subordinates, young man." Nell shook her head and stepped back, out of reach of Ezra and the telephone. "I won't do it."

"You're not listening to me. I said—"

"Ezra, when a man repeats himself, it's a sure sign he's run out of something worth saying."

Nell moved toward him and placed her pale hand on his arm. The dial tone began to sound as she looked up into his eyes through a shimmering of tears.

The fact he'd made her cry set Ezra's temples throbbing all over again. What sort of man had he become? Too many years away had turned him into someone he wasn't proud of.

He let the phone fall and cradled his grandmother in a hug, patting her iron gray curls. "I'm just trying to get you to listen to good sense. To me."

"Unfortunately, I heard every word," she whispered, her shaky voice barely audible over the annoying sound of the phone company's recorded message.

Ezra released her to reach for the phone. One glance at his grandmother and rage boiled. That woman, whoever she was, had hoodwinked his dear grandmother. It was written all over her face. Well, he would have none of it.

Ezra slammed the receiver down and attempted to glare at Nell, but his heart just wasn't in it. Instead he found himself praying the Lord would talk some sense into her if he could not.

"Young man," she began gently, "I love you like the grandchild I never had, but I love the Lord more. I intend to listen to the both of you as long as I live, but I'll only take orders from Him. Now you can like it, or you can keep quiet about it."

Several responses formulated in his mind. He chose to ignore them all in favor of a hug and a kiss for his favorite girl.

As he climbed on the plane, he prayed Granny Nell would heed his advice regarding the woman named Sophie Comeaux.

By the time he arrived back at his post, he'd decided Granny was too smart to do anything other than listen to him.

four

March 5, two years later

A surprise waited in Nell Landry's journal this lovely spring morning. Rather than a blank page ready for her to write down whatever the Lord wanted to say to her, Nell beheld the most beautiful piece of art she'd seen in ages.

Just below the spot where yesterday she'd recorded a passage from the book of Mark, a sweet kitten with short whiskers sat atop an apple-shaped cookie jar.

"After my time with the Lord, I'll have to go next door to get the artist's autograph."

Nell exchanged her favorite pink slippers for a pair of sneakers, then walked next door to find the twins in the backyard helping their mother. As the cowbell on the garden gate rattled, Sophie Comeaux looked up from her work.

"Sophie, sweetheart," Nell called, "may I borrow the artist of this fine-looking kitty?"

Her dear neighbor looked up from her work to frown. "Girls, have you been scribbling in Miss Nell's books again?"

"Don't scold them, dear. You know I encourage them to leave me little notes. Besides, this time they've been doing the Lord's work. One day you'll see that I'm telling the truth."

While Sophie gave her a doubtful look, Nell ignored the protest of her old joints to settle on the step beside Chloe, the elder and more bold of the twins. Like as not, the culprit had been Amanda, but this one generally acted as spokesperson for the pair.

"You're wearing our favorite apron," Amanda said.

She looked down at the apron tied around her waist. Habit made her reach for an apron each day, even when the amount of housework she accomplished didn't warrant a decent dust rag, much less an apron.

No, she wore this one more for the smile it gave her than any convenience or protection for her clothing. Made of little handkerchiefs sent by her grandson from his visits around the world, most of the squares had a verse from scripture to accompany the pretty picture and name of the location where Ezra purchased it.

Long after she laid the project aside, the girls had found the apron and insisted they complete it together. The lace and cotton concoction now sported twelve verses written in three different handwritings.

The leftover hankies were sprayed with a dab of perfume from the bottle on her dresser. One resided with each member of the little band of women at 421 Riverside Avenue. She'd shown the girls how to dab the cologne just so to make the scent last. She'd even made a note to herself to buy each of the Comeaux ladies their own bottle of their specially chosen scent next Christmas.

Amanda slid between her and the journal to rest her head on Nell's chest. While Chloe was bold and fearless, this one was a cuddler.

Nell kissed the top of her head and patted down a dark curl. "Now, about this drawing of yours. The last time I saw a picture of a kitty this beautiful was in a museum over in New Orleans. Came all the way from Italy, it did, and was over a hundred years old to boot." She winked at Amanda. "Almost as old as I am."

"It's a bunny, Miss Nell, and her name's Hoppy."

Funny how the girl quickly corrected the species of the animal but easily accepted the fact that Nell could be nearing the century mark. In truth, come winter she'd be seventy-six, but she was thankful the Lord had seen fit to keep her strong and fit. Well, except for that old flu bug. Still, nothing but a twinge now and then to remind her she was no longer in her prime.

She handed Amanda the journal. "Hoppy. Well now, that's a fine name for a bunny. Would you mind writing it up there over his head?"

"Her head," Amanda corrected. "Hoppy's a girl. Want me to sign my name, too?"

"How did you guess?"

"Because you always ask me to sign my name after I draw you a picture."

She touched the girl's tiny nose. "Do I now?"

"Yes, only this time I forgot."

Nell caught sight of Chloe just before the dear girl settled with a flop beside Amanda in her lap. Pain shot from her toenails to her teeth and back again, but Nell refused to react. She'd smart a bit before bedtime, but she'd never admit it to anyone.

Right now Nell preferred nothing more than to sit in the afternoon sun with her girls. She'd worry about her arthritis when she found the time.

Their mother looked as if she were about to scold them for being less than gentle with their guest. She gave Sophie a wink, then gathered the girls into her arms. "The only thing better than one baby in this old lap is two of them, especially on a fine spring day. I can't recall when I've felt so blessed. If Ezra were here, my family would be complete."

"Miss Nell," Sophie said, "you're the one doing the blessing."

"Oh, pshaw. This old lady's nothing but a bother." She tickled Amanda's tummy, then reached for Chloe to do the same. The girls giggled for a moment; then Chloe held her hands out toward the journal. "My turn."

Sweet Amanda gave up the book to her sister without complaint. What a pleasant child. As a youngster, Ezra had been more like Chloe, daring and bold, some days overstepping the bounds of propriety and other days racing past them at high speed. On occasion, however, he'd showed his softer side.

Sadly she was probably the only person who'd ever seen it.

"See—I drew a picture, too." Chloe turned the pages, and,

sure enough, a pink elephant waited to be found a few weeks down the road.

"Oh, that is absolutely the most gorgeous elephant I've ever seen. Looks just like the one I saw in New Orleans once. Well," she said slowly, "maybe not exactly."

" 'Cause it wasn't pink?" Amanda asked.

"That's right," Nell said. "It was purple." When the girls howled with laughter, she added a quick, "You don't believe me?"

"No," they said in unison.

"Well now, that's a fine thing to say. Until I met you two, I'd never heard of a pink Christmas tree, but I believed *you* when you said they existed."

She smiled at the memory of last Christmas's surprise, an overlarge holiday gift with limbs and needles painted a shocking pink by one of her former boarders over at Latagnier Auto Works. If only she'd specified a smaller tree. Something that would have fit through the door without cracking the glass.

Dear Alonzo had gone all out, as was his nature. He fetched the biggest Christmas tree he could find to the paint shop where his men made short order of turning it into the exact color of the twins' bedroom wall.

Somehow she'd managed to get the tree inside and covered with ribbons and bows before the girls came home from school. What a treat it was to see their faces. She thought of them every time she looked at the crack she'd made in the stained glass over the door.

If one looked carefully, traces of the pink wood chips were still left on the front lawn after the tree had been trimmed down to size.

Well, no matter. The Lord never made her perfect or a carpenter. She was thankful He was both.

"So," Nell said, "if Christmas trees can be pink, why can't elephants be purple?"

A fit of giggles later, the girls were quizzing Nell about the elephants and the range of colors of the animals she saw. Amanda ran in for construction paper while Chloe got the markers. In short order they began to crank out elephants in all sorts of sizes and colors.

"What was the name of the place where you saw it, Miss Nell?" Amanda asked.

"Oh, dear, that was so long ago. Honestly I don't remember." She paused. "You know who would remember though?"

Chloe looked up from her attempt at writing her last name in cursive handwriting. "Who?"

"My grandson, Ezra. I know I've told him that story many times. He probably knows the details better than I."

"Who's Ezra?" Amanda asked.

Nell looked past the twins to Sophie, who now toiled over a patch of weeds in the easternmost corner of her garden. "Someone very special," Nell said. "Special like your mama." She returned her attention to the precious little ones. "I want you girls to promise me something. Can you do that?"

When they finished nodding, she continued. "I'm going to leave this book here with you. I want you to fill it with pretty pictures."

Again they nodded.

"That's wonderful. Now when it's finished—that is, when all the pages are decorated nice and pretty—I want you to keep it safe until my grandson comes, and then I want you to give it to my grandson as a gift from the three of us. The only thing I ask is that you don't take out anything I've already put in and you don't color over the pages I've written on. Can you do that?"

"Yes, ma'am," they said in unison.

Contentment. Nothing but the Lord and little children could offer it. Leastwise, it seemed so the older she got.

Sophie looked up to swipe at her forehead with the back of her hand. Their gazes met, and Nell offered her a smile. "How about I go fetch us some iced tea in those fancy glasses I keep in the top cabinet? I bet I've got some fresh cookies in the apple jar, too."

Her neighbor shook her head. "Please don't go to any

trouble, Miss Nell. You're just getting over the flu. Why don't I run in and grab us a snack so you don't have to get up?"

"That pesky flu bug is last week's news, young lady. I'm fit as a fiddle." She looked down at the girls. "Unless I forget, I'll fetch my bottle of perfume, too."

"I'll go get my handkerchief, Miss Nell. I keep it under my pillow," Chloe said.

Amanda scrambled up to follow her sister inside. "Me, too," she called.

"Miss Nell, I don't think I have ever seen two girls as excited about handkerchiefs before." Sophie chuckled before going back to her weeding.

"Well, in my day, handkerchiefs were essential. I'm pleased they've taken to my custom of spraying a bit of fragrance—"

"To make it last," Sophie said along with Nell. "Miss Nell, will I embarrass you too much if I tell you once again what a blessing you are to us? Why, if it weren't for you, the girls and I wouldn't have a decent roof over our heads. Come to think of it, there probably would be no 'girls and I.' "

"Oh, honey, I'm the blessed one. Now let me go get the tea and those cookies before my old mind forgets what I promised to do."

Both hands gripping the rails, Nell rose. Ignoring the black spots dancing before her eyes, she dusted off the seat of her double-knit slacks and waited for the silly vertigo to ease up. While the flu bug had bitten her hard, the lingering symptoms were proving even more troublesome.

Judson Villare—grandson of Doc Villare who delivered her and saw her through the ailments of childhood—was a good Christian man and a fine cardiologist, even if he did start out his career as her paperboy, but she had to wonder if he'd misread her file. The dear fellow seemed to think her ticker was on the blink.

Of course she'd tell no one about this. They'd just make a fuss.

No sense in raising a ruckus about something that couldn't

be helped. What with Sophie being a nurse and all, well, it just seemed the sweet girl worried too much about her anyway. Far too much to think of her own self. No, she was the one who needed someone to worry after her. A husband, perhaps.

Nell paused a second to smile at the thought of Sophie's little family with a man added to it. *Oh, I like that idea.*

She chuckled as she made her way to the gate with care, then walked around to open her back door when the pesky pain hit her again. It subsided as quickly as it arrived, then returned with full force.

Nell slid inside on legs she could barely feel. The screen door slammed. The pain worsened.

Reaching for the cabinet where she kept her pills, Nell gasped. Her hand landed on the Bible sitting on the counter.

"This, too, shall pass," she managed as she cradled the precious book to her aching chest. "And if it doesn't, I'll just call Judson. He'll know what to do. I don't have time to feel bad."

But this time it didn't pass. Instead the pain burned white hot, until the brilliant light and soft, insistent voice chased it away.

five

March 9

Sophie Comeaux hid her tears behind Nell Landry's white cotton handkerchief. Holding the soft fabric to her nose, she closed her eyes and inhaled the faint scent of perfume that even the washing machine had failed to remove. Without looking, she knew an image of the Raffles Hotel in Singapore waited in a fold of the fabric.

She opened her eyes and smiled, remembering the woman instead of mourning the loss as she stepped out of the little church into the bright afternoon light. Blinking to adjust to the change from the dark interior of the church, she ran smack into a wall covered in the navy fabric of a marine's dress uniform.

"Excuse me, miss," he said softly, almost absently, as if he'd been the cause of the collision.

The voice rumbled through her mind and set it racing. She peered up into a pair of coffee-colored eyes fringed with thick lashes, soft eyes set in a hard face.

A soldier's face.

The thought shook free a loose memory, and for a moment the world froze. An icy film, tiny cracks in a frosty glass, began to appear as slowly, painfully, a memory unfolded.

Then Nell's words came to her. "Remember it's in His hands." Sophie managed a weak smile as the memory fell away and a warmth flooded her heart.

"You dropped this," the marine said, although his square jaw barely moved.

Sophie jammed her mind into the present and merely shivered, rather than allow the violent trembling to overtake

32

her. "I'm sorry," she mumbled and pressed past him to stumble toward her car.

"Ma'am?"

Standing tall and stiff, the soldier wore his rank with an air of loss. From his blue black hair to the shine on his medals, he looked as if he'd not intended to be where he stood. It made no sense; yet it made perfect sense.

Sophie looked down at the object in the marine's hand. Nell's handkerchief. Somehow it must have fallen. Pure white with only a smudge of mascara, the fabric stood in stark contrast to the deep tan of his fingers and the crisp navy of his uniform.

"Here." He thrust the lace-trimmed cloth toward her, his gaze set on the handkerchief rather than on her. "My grandmother used to carry these," he said softly. "Always smelled like perfume."

"To make it last," she whispered.

"Yes." Their gazes met and locked. "Here," he repeated.

"I, um, thank you," she stammered. Sophie reached for the precious memory of Nell resting in the marine's palm, and their fingers touched. For a split second an arc of electricity stung her, and she snatched the cloth back.

"Excuse me," she said as she tucked the handkerchief in her purse and fumbled for the keys to give her fingers something to do and her mind something to think about. By the time she found them and let herself inside the car, the marine had gone.

"Strange," she said under her breath as she eased the car into traffic and headed home. "He seemed so familiar."

six

"Sophie, are you sitting down?"

Sophie Comeaux let off the brake, allowing the minivan to move into the next available spot in front of Latagnier Elementary School. "It's three thirty on a Monday afternoon, Bree. Of course I'm sitting. I'm in the van at the girls' school. Why?"

"Well, you know how I was supposed to go by your house and turn off the sprinkler this morning?"

Her cell phone in one hand, she picked at a piece of lint decorating the knee of her scrubs with her other. "Bree Jackson, don't tell me you're just now turning it off. My yard must look like Lake Pontchartrain."

"Hey, I forgot a file and had to run by the office before I went to court, so that threw me off. Besides, you're the one who left for the hospital before you finished watering the lawn *again*. I'm just the good neighbor and best friend who takes care of her favorite nurse."

"And your favorite nurse is very thankful to her favorite attorney and neighbor." The bell sounded, signaling the end of the school day and the last minutes of silence in Sophie's van. "So my yard *doesn't* look like Lake Pontchartrain?"

"Actually it kind of does, but that's not the point. Is there anything you meant to tell me? Maybe something important?"

The school's doors blew open, and a wave of students burst forth. Somehow they all fell into orderly lines for bus riders and car riders. She recognized a few of the students as friends of Chloe and Amanda, but so far the girls had not emerged.

Strange, the twins were usually the first ones out the door.

"Soph, stick with me here. This is important."

She shifted her attention from "mom mode" to "friend mode" for a moment. "What was that, Bree? You know I was only teasing about the yard. I guess I'll have to spring for one of those timers. I hate to see Miss Nell's trumpet vines drooping."

"Forget the yard a minute, would you? It's just that if you were planning something as big as this, one would think you would have called your best friend before you. . ."

The girls emerged into the afternoon sun and raced for the van. Chloe won, beating Amanda by a hairbreadth to take the front seat. With both chattering at once, it was hard to hear Bree.

"Hang on a sec. Let me get the girls settled." She set the phone in her lap and turned to watch the girls slip into their seat belts.

"Slowly now," she said. "One of you tell me what's so exciting."

Chloe sighed. "You tell it, Amanda."

Amanda echoed her sister's sigh. "Chloe and me—"

"Chloe and I," Sophie corrected.

The younger twin nodded. "Chloe and I won this." Amanda thrust a large brown envelope with the Latagnier Elementary logo toward Sophie.

"On account of we're citizens of the month, we get free ice cream," Chloe said. "Miss Robbins said she couldn't pick between us so we both got to be it."

Good thing the teacher's not around at bedtime. She might change her mind.

"That's wonderful, girls." Sophie removed the contents of the envelope. Two certificates for free junior-sized cones at the Dip Cone landed atop a pair of official-looking documents proclaiming her daughters as model citizens of Latagnier Elementary. "Oh, we'll have to frame these."

"Helloo." The muffled word came from her phone.

Bree.

"Oh, I'm so sorry," Sophie said. "I'm going to have to call you back. Seems as though the girls have been named citizens of the month for September. Looks like a celebration is in order."

"Where's the party? Girl, you and I have to talk, and I mean like *right now.*"

"Sounds serious." She cast a glance at the girls to be sure they'd settled properly into their seats, then returned her attention to Bree. "I'm about to pull out of the car line. How about you meet us at the Dip Cone in fifteen minutes?"

The mention of Latagnier's favorite ice cream shop caused a squeal of delight and another round of conversation that lasted until the van began to move. After that, the girls were too busy waving to their friends and shouting through the open windows to speak to their boring mom.

Funny how nice it felt to be thought of as a boring mom. It certainly hadn't always been that way. But then the girls were a precious blessing who came along when she least expected and most needed them. She was hard-pressed to remember her life before Chloe and Amanda came to live with her.

And before they all came to live under the same roof as Nell Landry.

The thought of Nell, so recently gone home to be with the Lord, sent a shaft of fresh pain coursing through her. Only her assurance that someday she would be reunited with the dear lady kept Sophie from feeling completely lost.

It was hard to believe the precious soul had already been gone six months. Most days it felt as though Nell would come padding across the porch in her favorite pink slippers at any moment.

A piercing squeal of what had better be delight jolted Sophie from her reverie. "All right, settle down a bit so I can get us out of here in one piece, okay?"

Somehow Sophie managed to navigate her way out of the school traffic and onto the broad avenue that led from

Latagnier Elementary to the downtown district where the road turned to a narrow cobbled thoroughfare. She negotiated the dips and hollows in the old road, slowing to turn into the parking lot of the only downtown business that never seemed to lack for customers: the Dip Cone.

With the spaces out front already full, Sophie turned the van into the empty space next door where a parking lot had been carved from land that used to host a beautiful old home.

"Me first," both girls called at once as the doors opened and they sprinted for the double doors, propped wide open to allow the fresh breeze inside.

Mr. Arceneaux looked up as the girls burst in, then smiled at Sophie before attending to their orders. Out of the corner of her eye, she saw Bree's shiny white convertible sports car pull into the spot beside her van.

"A diet soda for me and a double dip of pistachio with whipped cream and a cherry for Bree," she said as she counted her money and set it on the counter.

While Mr. Arceneaux set about preparing the lady lawyer's favorite treat, the girls skipped out back to a table beneath the tattered red-and-white-striped umbrella. Bree hit the floor running, her expensive pumps tapping out a quick rhythm on Mr. Arceneaux's ancient linoleum floor. Before Sophie could say hello, Bree grabbed her arm.

"Some friend you are." Bree gave Sophie a sideways look. "I mean, *really*."

"Hey, I invited you to the celebration as soon as I knew there was going to be one, and I even paid." She accepted the dish from Mr. Arceneaux and handed it to her friend. "See, one Bree Jackson special, extra whipped cream."

Bree seemed oblivious, her attention fixed on Sophie. "Talk, girl," she said, the collection of silver bracelets jingling on her left hand. "Where are you moving, and why didn't you tell me before Latagnier Realty put a sign in your yard?"

seven

Sophie pulled the van to a stop at the curb and shut off the engine. There it was, just as Bree said. Square in the middle of her side of the yard sat a red, white, and blue Latagnier Realty sign advertising a house—her house—for sale.

"Mommy," Chloe whispered, eyes wide, "didn't Miss Nell tell us we could live here as long as we want?"

"Of course she did, sweetheart," Sophie answered. "Surely this must be some mistake. After all, the other half is empty so maybe someone thought. . ." Neither girl seemed to be buying the excuse. "You know what? I'm going to call Latagnier Realty and tell them they've got the wrong yard."

The statement placated them, for the moment anyway. Putting on a false smile, Sophie waited until the girls were engrossed in their homework before she punched in the numbers to the real estate office.

"Four twenty-one Riverside Avenue?" the woman repeated once she'd taken down the information. "Yes, that's a new listing."

Sophie sank into the nearest chair and repeated the address. "Are you sure? Could there be some mistake?"

"Mistake?" The woman's friendly voice turned curt. "I hardly think so. I did the paperwork myself. Is there a problem with the property?"

"Only that it's mine," she managed.

The woman chuckled. "Only if you're related to the man whose attorney's signature appears on the documents."

Sophie's fingers tightened around the receiver as the woman's words sank in. "What man?"

"You should know, honey. You're living in his house," she said, frost dangling from each word. "If you're having a domestic issue with your husband, you'd better talk to him about it. I'm not a marriage counselor." The ice cracked, and the line went dead.

When Sophie replaced the receiver on the cradle, she almost wished she hadn't. The girls, who had been eerily quiet during her phone conversation, began to question her, both speaking at the same time. Numb, she waved them away.

Lord, what do I do now?

When an immediate answer failed to appear, Sophie cleared her throat and took a deep breath. She let it out slowly and gathered both girls into her lap.

While Chloe snuggled against her shoulder, Amanda looked up intently, a light spattering of what looked like yellow paint dotting her right cheek. Sophie reached for a kitchen towel and dabbed it against her tongue before swiping at the little girl's face.

"Mommy, do you want to sell our house?" Amanda asked.

"Yeah, Mommy, you don't want to move, do you? I like it here," Chloe added.

Two sets of precious brown eyes stared in her direction. Again Sophie petitioned the Lord for an answer. Again He remained silent.

Finally she found her voice. "Miss Nell gave us this house." She kissed Amanda on the cheek. "It's our home, and we're not leaving it."

Chloe gave Amanda a high five. "Yippee! Let's go take down the ugly sign."

"Hold it," Sophie said, shifting Amanda off her lap. "Until I know more about what's going on here, we're going to have to leave the sign in the yard."

Amanda glared accusingly. "Sarah Josten's mommy and daddy sold their house, and she told me she had to keep her room clean because strangers had to walk all over the place. They even looked in the closets."

"I don't want strangers looking in my closet," Chloe whined. "And I don't want to sell our house."

Amanda tugged on the tail of Sophie's scrubs and stuck out her lower lip in a pout. "Mommy, strangers are bad." She shook her head, dislodging a dark curl from the ponytail Sophie had painstakingly tied with a red bow that morning. "I don't want strangers in my room."

"Mommy!" Amanda's cry turned from a whine to a high-pitched squeal in lightning speed, nearly obliterating the sound of the doorbell.

Temporarily distracted, both girls raced for the door, most likely to tell their tale of woe to one of the neighbor girls. Grateful for even a moment's relief, Sophie leaned back against the chair and closed her eyes.

Tiredness snaked up her spine and settled into her bones. An image of Nell rose unbidden in her mind.

"You gave us this house," she whispered to her. "At least I thought you did."

True, she hadn't received paperwork on the place, but the letter Nell had written said it all. She wanted this half of the house to be the place Sophie lived with the girls.

"Mommy!" Amanda shouted a second later, shattering the picture in her mind.

She mustered the strength to open her eyes. "Yes?" she called.

"There's a man here," Amanda said.

Great. Dealing with pesky salesmen was never high on her list of things to do, but now the task seemed even more impossible than ever.

"Tell him we don't allow solicitors, then politely close the door."

She heard Amanda try, with Chloe's help, to repeat her statement. Twice they stumbled over the word "solicitor," causing Sophie to grin despite the cloud of doubt about the house situation. What would she do without her precious girls? Even in the dark times, they managed to shine a little light.

A deep rumble of unintelligible words caused her to realize the girls had failed to make their point. She climbed to her feet and shuffled down the hall toward the door feeling older than dirt.

As she rounded the corner, the door swung open to reveal a man in a dark, rumpled suit and faded blue tie. In his hand he carried a slip of paper.

"Miss Sophie Comeaux of 421 Riverside Avenue?" he asked, pushing thick-lensed glasses higher on his nose.

"Yes."

He extended his hand as if to shake hers, then pressed the paper into her palm. "Consider yourself served," he said as he beat a hasty retreat.

"Served?" She looked down at the paper in her hand. "With what?"

Her gaze fell to the words on the page, and her heart, what was left of it, sank.

"Nell didn't intend for this to happen." Sophie straightened her shoulders and reached for the phone. "Back to homework, girls. I'm going to make a quick call to Auntie Bree." She punched two on speed dial and waited while her best friend's voice came on the line. "Hey, Bree, know how you're always trying to fix me up with your cousin the real estate attorney? Well, I'd like his number, but don't get excited. This won't be a social call."

"So the sign wasn't a practical joke?"

Sophie let out a long breath. "I wish. Seems like some man has decided he owns this property and is intending to sell it."

"What man?"

"That's what I'd like your cousin to find out."

"Oh no, honey," Bree said. "Forget my cousin. I'm handling this one myself. What sort of documentation or affidavits do you have that will prove your property rights?"

"English, please."

Bree sighed. "Did Miss Nell give you anything in writing that would prove your case? Something that specifically gives the property to you?"

Sophie thought a second. "Nothing official like a deed or

anything, but she wrote a note on a Mother's Day card right after we moved in."

"What did it say?"

"Just that she intended us always to have a roof over our heads. She cited Psalm 68 in it, I believe."

"Did that include both sides of the house or just the half you're living in?"

"Well," Sophie said, "I don't remember her being specific about that. I guess I never thought about it."

"Did she sign it?" Bree asked.

"Well, she signed the card, and the note was right there above her name."

"And you've still got it?"

"In my Bible." She paused to shift the phone to the other ear. "Why?"

"Why?" Her friend chuckled. "It just became evidence. If Miss Nell intended you and the girls to live in that house, I doubt the state of Louisiana will go against her wishes."

"That's good news, Bree."

"Hang on to that thought, honey. It could be a long time before you get more good news." A phone rang in the background. "I need to dash, Soph. How about I treat you and the girls to pizza delivery tonight at my place while we go over this in detail? I'd really like to file a motion before the end of the week so we can set a hearing date. Once that's in line, I think we can put a hold on the sale, at least until the judge rules."

"That means the house will go off the market?"

"Temporarily," Bree said. "But you can remove the sign. Now, about dinner."

"I've got a better idea," Sophie said. "I'll make dinner if you'll come here instead. How does barbecue sound?"

"Considering you make the best ribs in the state of Louisiana, I am heading for the car. What can I bring?"

"How about a salad and a solution to my problem?"

eight

Ezra Landry's heart—what was left of it—sank.

The attorney assigned to him by the Marine Corps had never deemed it necessary to trek to the wilds of Java to see him. The fact that he now stood at attention, obviously waiting for permission to approach, did not bode well.

With the training that had long become habit, Ezra studied his visitor and drew an instant conclusion. Out of his element, this guy, and probably not much help beyond pushing a few papers and lighting the general's cigars.

The first lieutenant was slim and straight as a rail, and his dark hair and eyes stood in extreme contrast to the paleness of his skin and the shine of perspiration decorating his brow. Not an infantry attorney, his buddy Calvin Dubose's term for men like Calvin who preferred the battlefield to the courtroom and could easily transition between the two.

No doubt the man spent most of his days in a Virginia law library rather than seeing clients in this steamy, jungle-infested corner of the planet. On top of that, he looked about as nervous as a long-tailed cat in a room full of rocking chairs.

Ezra knew the reaction well.

It came with the position. The position that officially did not exist.

"Would you repeat what you just said?" He motioned for the lawyer to take a seat and watched as he complied. If any man could sit at attention, it was this one. He knew the type: Joe College with a need for structure. Perfect military lawyer. Probably showered, shaved, and ate all his meals at attention.

"Relax, soldier. No matter what you heard, I don't bite."

The lawyer turned up one corner of his mouth in what probably passed for a smile in his circles. "Of course, sir."

While the man detailed his plan to dispose of his grandmother's house, Ezra listened in silence. When he got to the part about the place being occupied, he held up his hand to stop him.

"You mean there *is* still someone living in my grandmother's house after all?"

The lawyer's spine stiffened. "Yes, sir." He opened a slim metal briefcase and extracted four sheets of paper. "One adult and two minors. Females, sir."

"Females." Ezra sucked in a slow breath and tried to digest the information.

"Let me get this straight. A woman and two children are living in my grandmother's house even after my grandmother's death?"

"Yes, sir. Half of it anyway. She has her mail sent to 421A."

"Name, please."

He consulted the papers before him, then thrust two of them toward Ezra. "One Sophia Rebecca Comeaux, age twenty-nine and legal adoptive parent to seven-year-old twins Chloe Rose and Amanda Grace Comeaux. Ms. Comeaux is an employee of Latagnier General Hospital in their neonatal unit, and the juveniles attend primary school. Second grade."

Could this be the woman Granny Nell spoke of? The coincidence was too strong to ignore, and yet he felt sure she would have heeded his advice and changed her mind about taking them in. She certainly hadn't mentioned anything about them in her letters.

Ezra swung his gaze to address his officially assigned lawyer.

"Do we know how long these females have been living in my late-grandmother's home?"

The attorney shook his head. "Not at this time, sir, although the necessary paperwork has been filed to begin the process of removing them. With your signed affidavit, I expect the papers have already been served."

"But in the meantime they reside under my grandmother's roof?"

The attorney swallowed hard. "They do, temporarily, at least."

He indicated for the man to continue his story, steepling his fingers as he gave the papers a cursory glance and listened to the lawyer drone on about probate requirements, residential sales agreements, and real estate law. While he pretended interest, the truth be known, he only meant to comply with the words in his grandmother's will.

In her cryptic writing, she had scribbled a hasty note at the bottom of the document she'd had drawn up a decade earlier. Dated only a few months before her death, it left no doubt in Ezra's mind as to how she wished to dispose of her estate. A copy of the amended document had been folded atop a shiny set of house keys and left for him in the vault of the State Bank of Louisiana, downtown branch.

At least that's what Calvin told him the last time they'd been in contact. If only he'd had the presence of mind to ask Calvin to handle the last of the details. Then he might have found out about the interlopers from a friend.

Ezra made a mental note to let the brass know that in any further legal matters his representation would come from Calvin Dubose, not some randomly assigned Ivy Leaguer.

You take everything else, but leave the house to the orphans, Ezra, she'd written, and that was exactly what he intended to do.

He smiled. While the house wasn't worth much, it would still make for a tidy donation to the local orphanage once it was sold.

While the lawyer continued to speak, Ezra picked up the legal document and read the first few lines. "Excuse me, soldier. What is your name?" He could have read it off the man's name tag, but he felt the need to hear him say it.

The lawyer looked flustered. "First Lieutenant Hawthorne, sir."

Ezra nodded. "First Lieutenant Hawthorne, has anyone bothered to ask Miss—what was her name?"

"Comeaux, sir."

Again he nodded. "Has anyone asked Miss Comeaux what she's doing in my grandmother's house?"

Attorney Hawthorne looked even more uncomfortable as he seemed to consider the question. "I don't believe so, sir," he finally said. "But she has been served with papers indicating there is a claim on the house in which she resides. A hearing was held and passed, due to your absence, but with your permission, I will file a motion and get this handled."

If a legal battle ensued, Calvin would handle the details. *Period.* The last thing he intended to do was leave something this important to a man he did not know. He stated this to the first lieutenant who, to Ezra's surprise, looked positively relieved.

Ezra rose to his full height, an advantage he rarely used in negotiations, and stared the lawyer down with his most intimidating look. To his credit, Hawthorne stared right back, although the sheen on his forehead had increased.

"Are you sure you want to tell me you can't remove three females from an unauthorized location?"

"No, sir," he said.

Easing into the chair, Ezra forced a smile. "Then you are saying you can?"

"No, sir," he repeated, his neck now a bright shade of red. "That's not what I'm saying at all, sir."

Their gazes met and locked. Slowly, never moving his from the attorney's, Ezra contemplated his words carefully.

"I'm going to give you thirty seconds." He drew a sharp breath. "And you're going to use that thirty seconds to help me understand what you're talking about," he said as he exhaled. "Are we clear?"

Hawthorne nodded. "Crystal clear, sir."

Ezra consulted his watch, then looked up at the lawyer. "Begin."

First Lieutenant Hawthorne held the metal case against his chest as if he were about to dodge bullets. "The thing is, sir, I *don't* like telling you I can't do what you wish. The truth is, this real estate matter has to go through the civilian courts, and these things take time, especially in Louisiana, which has a judicial system unlike any other state." He blinked, barely. "I *would* like to help further, but I have orders and—"

"What sort of orders?" Ezra leaned toward the lawyer and watched with satisfaction as the man cringed.

Slowly Hawthorne opened the case and extracted an envelope. He thrust it toward Ezra. "Orders to give you this and then forget I was here," he said, cutting his gaze to meet Ezra's briefly. "Sir," he added belatedly.

Ezra weighed the envelope in his palm and watched Hawthorne make good on his escape. As the sound of footsteps echoed in the corridor, Ezra spied the seal on the envelope and sank into his chair. Only one person had access to that seal.

Closing his eyes, Ezra willed himself to concentrate on the matter at hand. Whatever happened with Granny Nell's house could be sorted out later. He'd learned early on that distraction could kill faster than any of the enemy's weapons.

When he lifted the edge of the seal and read the letter inside, he knew he was a dead man. At least he might as well have been dead. The paper in front of him stated that until his legal matters back home were solved he was of no use to the department.

The distraction to him and the potential of publicity, however small, made him unfit for duty. Ezra threw the papers into the metal toolbox, then reached behind him to grab a match and strike it. As flame met paper, Ezra rose and headed for the door.

No need to watch his future burn. He'd be there in person to see that soon enough.

"Hawthorne," he called, then waited while the man did an about-face and marched back in his direction.

"Yes, sir?"

"One last thing. Write this number down." When the soldier had located pen and paper from his briefcase, Ezra dictated Calvin's number to him. "Major Calvin Dubose, Fourth Marine Division, Louisiana," he added for emphasis. "Tell him what you just told me. He will be handling the matter from here on out."

As a parting gift, Ezra gave the attorney a look he'd perfected in his short stint as a drill instructor back at Camp Lejeune, and the lieutenant went scurrying out the door. "Lord, what are You up to this time?" he whispered.

nine

Ezra's civilian shirt itched around the collar, and his jeans refused to hold a proper crease. No matter, for he had no intention of making a good impression on the trespassing females currently camping in his house.

Granny Nell's house, he corrected as he turned the midsized, nondescript rental car onto Riverside Avenue and parked in a rare empty space within sight of the property. He shifted into PARK and removed his handkerchief to mop his brow. Even with the air-conditioning, the temperature hovered higher than a Javanese jungle in midafternoon.

Anywhere else, September would have ushered in at least a hint of fall, but not here in Latagnier. At least not today.

"Buck up, Marine," he said as he adjusted the vent so the air would blow cold on his face. "This is just another mission. Just one more assignment in a long list of assignments."

And once he took care of the personal business that was drawing too much attention to him, he could go back to his old life. That much of a promise he'd wrested from his commanding officer, although General Scanlon had been vague about an exact date or location for his return.

The last guy on their under-the-radar team who left to take care of personal business never came back. He'd heard the man was put on desk duty in New Mexico. The reason: Too many people saw him and remembered him.

In their line of work, that could mean a mission compromised. Could that be what was on the general's mind?

Ezra shrugged off the concern that came with the general's ambiguous response. "Keep your mind on the mission," he muttered as he thumped the file on the seat beside him. "How hard can it be to evict a hospital employee and two elementary school students?"

A scan of the terrain revealed few significant changes in his grandmother's house. The doors now matched, both wearing a fresh coat of black paint. The crack still shimmered in the stained glass above 421A, but that was the only flaw he could find.

In fact, the old place never looked better. A potted palm stood between the matching front doors, flowers in feminine colors arranged around its base. On either corner of the porch, a hanging fern's fronds swung in the warm breeze. The only thing missing was the FOR SALE sign, temporarily removed until the judge ruled.

Last night upon arrival, Calvin assured him the issue would be settled in two weeks, three at the most. At this point Ezra didn't know how he would make it two days here.

Life on the edge suited him. Loafing on Cal's lounge chair with mindless American reality shows on the television and fast food in his belly was not his idea of how to live. "Give me a jungle, a mission, and a blanket under the stars any day."

Ezra sighed and mopped his neck. Spending any amount of time in south Louisiana in the warm months had to be the closest thing to spending an eternity without the Lord. It certainly was the same temperature.

And the mosquitoes and humidity? Only the devil himself could have come up with those.

Yet he had happy memories associated with this place and season. How many summers had he spent sitting with his nose pointed toward Granny Nell's silver metal floor fan, only blinking when the cool breeze forced his dry eyes to shut. And, oh, the ice cream he ate—homemade vanilla ice cream churned right on that porch until his arm ached.

For a kid from the other side of the river, he'd done all right. He might have been born in the little village of Algiers across the Mississippi from New Orleans, but his home was here in the heart of Cajun country on Riverside Avenue.

Always had been; always would be.

"I hope those orphans appreciate this." As soon as the words were out, he cringed. "I'm sorry, Lord. That sounded awful."

He leaned against the headrest and jammed the handkerchief into his shirt pocket. "Let me try that again, God. Granny Nell gave me this house to provide for the widows and orphans, and that's what I'm going to do."

Ezra slunk down in the seat and reached for the sunglasses resting on the console. As a secondary measure, he pushed the brim on his hat lower. For a moment he regretted his decision not to involve Calvin in this phase of the mission.

One pint-sized female wearing a red polka-dot dress and braids emerged from 421A with some sort of fabric toy draped over her right arm. A second female of similar size and coloring clothed in yellow followed, carrying a small pail and shovel.

The pair proceeded to the patch of flowers on the southern-most perimeter of the property amid some amount of discussion. He couldn't hear the words over the roar of the air conditioner, but the conversation seemed to revolve around the ownership of the spatula-sized shovel.

A moment later a third juvenile, this one smaller in a jeans outfit accessorized with a straw cowboy hat and green galoshes, walked across the street and onto the premises to enter the fray, wrestling the shovel away from the warring parties.

Ezra watched while the girl with the shovel negotiated some sort of peace treaty with the others. Before he could blink twice, the trio were sitting happily together and laughing as they took turns digging.

"They could use a negotiator like her up in Washington," he muttered.

The door swung open once again, and out stepped a woman far too young looking to be the parent of a school-age brood. Nothing in the file the lieutenant gave him indicated another adult was in the household, so the female in the pink T-shirt and white shorts with matching pink flip-flops must be the babysitter.

The file.

He opened it and hid behind its manila cover. As he alternated between studying the enemy on Granny Nell's porch and the first page of the file, a dull ache began to form between his brows.

The woman stepped to the edge of the porch and began to speak. From his vantage point, her lips moved, but the words were lost in the whoosh and hum of the air-conditioner. He briefly considered trying to read her lips, then realized there was only one thing to do.

Groaning, he reached to shut off the air conditioning, then discreetly cracked the passenger-side window an inch. Instantly a wave of heat hit him. So did the pain between his brows.

"But, Mommy!" the one in yellow called.

Mommy?

Ezra took another look at the slender woman now kneeling alongside the girls. With her glossy dark ponytail and fresh-scrubbed face, she looked no more than a decade older than any of them.

She'd left her pink flip-flops on the porch and now held court barefoot in the dirt with a trio of pigtailed jesters dancing around her. As the woman reached to flatten the loose earth around a patch of white flowers, no queen ever looked so fair, even with a noticeable smudge of dirt on the side of her shorts.

So this was Sophie Comeaux. Funny how she'd never quite looked like this in his mind. No, the interloper who refused to return Granny Nell's home to its rightful owner had always resembled more of a shrew than someone's sweetheart.

"Buck up, Marine," he said on the release of a long breath. A bead of sweat trickled down his temple, and he ignored it. "Just another mission. Sometimes the enemy surprises you."

The girl in red met his gaze and stared a moment too long

for his liking. Another five minutes in the car and he'd be toast.

Either he had to confront the enemy head on, or he had to retreat. Given the fact he wanted—no, *needed*—to have this situation under control, he chose the former.

Throwing the car door open, he stepped out onto the uneven sidewalk. In his estimation, a direct approach would get the job done.

Tossing his hat and shades on the seat, he let the door slam and palmed the keys. "Sophie Comeaux?"

Four sets of eyes swung their attention in his direction. "Yes, I'm Sophie," their leader said as she rose. "Who wants to know?"

Great. Now what?

He waited for a blue sedan to pass, then sprinted across the street to thrust his hand in her direction. "Ezra," he said. "Ezra Landry."

&

Ezra Landry. Nell's grandson, the marine.

Great. Now what?

When Nell's grandson missed the hearing and the FOR SALE sign was removed from the yard, she'd felt as if she'd won a well-deserved reprieve. The silence that marked the days since then enforced that feeling.

It had been more wishful thinking than anything else; she knew it, but still she'd hoped for a long period of peace before the next battle with Nell's grandson.

And from the looks of this man, he'd survived a battle or two before.

Sophie clapped her hands together to knock the dirt off, then accepted Ezra's handshake, all the while staring into eyes that frightened her terribly. Oh, they were nice enough, almond shaped and fringed in thick black lashes, and his cheekbones beneath them looked to be cut from granite and covered in skin the color of café au lait. He might have been a handsome man if he smiled.

No, it was not the appearance of those eyes, that face, the man that frightened her. It was what lay behind them that sent a jolt of fear through her.

Somewhere in the mahogany depths, his eyes spoke a warning. This was not a man used to obstacles in his path.

And he was a marine. Old feelings threatened. She pushed them away.

Before she came out to call the girls, she'd been reading the story of Samson at the kitchen table. Funny, but this man reminded her of the biblical figure from her daily devotional. Well, except for the hair.

She broke the handshake as soon as was appropriate, then took a deep breath and let it out slowly. The girls now stood beside her, each staring with the same look she, too, must be wearing.

"Girls," she said with forced calm, "this is Mr. Landry. He is Miss Nell's grandson. Say hello to him."

"Hello," Chloe said reluctantly. Caroline, who lived down the street, repeated the greeting with a similar lack of enthusiasm.

Then Amanda stepped forward. At first it seemed as though Sophie's quieter child would echo her more-outgoing sister's response. Instead she motioned for the man to come down to her level. To Sophie's surprise, he did just that.

He wasn't an overly large man, but he did have a certain presence. Kneeling before her younger daughter, Ezra Landry still seemed intimidating.

Funny, but Amanda did not seem to notice. Rather, her daughter seemed to peer into the face of the stranger with something akin to curiosity. He ran his fingers through his military-style haircut and let out a sigh.

"What's your name?"

Before she spoke, she touched his hand, then worked her expression into a frown. "I'm Amanda Comeaux. Are you the man who makes my mommy cry at night?"

ten

"All right, Amanda," Sophie said quickly as she whirled the girl around to face her. "That's enough. It's time for Caroline to go home." She turned to address the twins. "Why don't you two say good-bye to your friend and go get washed up for supper?"

"But, Mommy, we were planting flowers and—"

"That's enough, Chloe." She gave the older twin "the look."

"Yes, Mommy," Chloe said. " 'Bye, Caroline. Race you to the sink, Amanda."

"Be sure you move the Bible off the counter before you turn the water on, please."

"I will," Amanda called as the screen door opened with a squeal. " 'Bye, Caroline."

"No, I will," Chloe said. "You always drop everything."

"I do not."

Off went two sets of dusty feet heading toward the kitchen she'd just scrubbed. The door slammed twice, most likely jarring loose the wreath of dried sunflowers and daisies she'd hung this morning. And yet that was the least of her problems.

Sophie watched the object of her thoughts rise to his full height, then dust off the knees of his jeans. When they finally met her stare, those determined eyes seemed a bit less intense, although no less purposeful.

"Cute kids," he said. "That all you've got, just those two?"

"Yes," she said slowly.

He nodded. "Cute kids."

"So you said."

The Landry fellow brushed something off his starched shirtsleeve and seemed in no hurry. "Guess I did," he said.

"Yes, you did. You know, a wise and dear friend of mine used to say that when one begins to repeat oneself, that is a sure indicator there is nothing left to say."

His gaze collided with hers, and Sophie resisted the urge to take a step backward. Rather, she stood her ground because it was just that: *her ground.*

Sophie squared her shoulders and prepared to end the politeness if necessary. Whatever it took, Ezra Landry needed to go back to wherever he came from. Preferably permanently.

"Look, I know you're Nell's grandson, but why are you here?"

"As you said, I *am* Nell's grandson." Ezra looked past her to grin. "And by virtue of that relationship, I am here to reclaim *my* house."

"Well, Mr. *Landry.*" Sophie took care in pronouncing both syllables of his last name as she watched his smile fade. "I had a relationship with Nell, too. And I wonder which of us had the closer relationship."

He quirked a dark brow but said nothing.

"Remind me." She paused for effect. "When was the last time you saw your grandmother? Alive, I mean?" The moment she said the words, she wanted to reel them back in. Sophie was a lot of things, but cruel was not one of them. "I'm sorry. That was terribly rude of me. I—"

"Hey. I might not have been around much the last few years, but at least I'm not trying to steal from the elderly."

Sophie's breath froze in her throat, and she forced herself to blink. *Steal from the elderly? What an awful man.*

"You have no idea what you're saying, Mr. Landry. I started as her home-health nurse when I was with the county. She and I developed a friendship, and she sort of took me under her wing." When his expression remained skeptical, she pressed on. "Nell *wanted* me to live next door to her. She practically *begged* me to, in fact. Said I'd never be able to finalize my adoption of the girls without a better job and a permanent home, and she couldn't let that happen."

"Did she now?"

"Yes, she did, and besides that, she gave me the courage to finish my schooling and go for a job at the hospital. She also gave me a place to live." Sophie paused for effect. "The operative word here," she said slowly, "is *gave*. I tried paying her rent, but she returned my checks and gave my cash to the church. Finally I gave up and added the amount I would have paid for rent to my monthly tithe."

His posture went rigid. "Can you prove that?"

"Prove what? That Nell wanted the house to go to me?" When he nodded, she returned the gesture. "I have a note from her stating this. Would that satisfy you?"

"Did it satisfy the courts?"

It hadn't—at least not yet. Bree said the legal wrangling would go on until Ezra Landry came forward to defend his claim.

Some provision was made for property claims that went undefended, but she hadn't quite grasped the details of it. The question of what Nell intended for the empty half of the house also remained unanswered.

Indeed, Sophie and the girls were temporarily in limbo, but they weren't there alone. The Lord was with them.

"I asked a question, Mrs. Comeaux."

Sophie swung her gaze to meet his. "That's *Miss* Comeaux. And as to your question, the litigation is ongoing."

Silently she congratulated herself for remembering the phrase. The term seemed lost on the man standing on her sidewalk, however.

The vague sounds of two girlish voices raised in what seemed like an argument drifted toward her on the hot breeze. A squeal followed, then silence. The silence worried her almost as much as the direction of her discussion with the Landry fellow.

He lifted his stare to offer what seemed like a challenge. "I wonder if you realize what you're doing, *Miss* Comeaux."

Sophie directed her imagination away from thoughts of the many possible messes she might be helping the girls clean up as soon as the Landry fellow was gone. "What *I'm* doing?" she echoed. "What do you mean?"

Was it her imagination, or did the man's shoulders seem a

bit broader, his posture a bit straighter? "I understand that a woman in your situation might resort to extraordinary means to keep a roof over her head and money in the bank. But. . ." He paused to glance behind her. "But I'm afraid you've chosen the wrong old lady to scam."

"Scam?" Oh, those were fighting words. She swallowed the caustic response that teased her tongue and took a deep breath, letting it out slowly. "How dare you arrive out of nowhere after paying your grandmother absolutely no attention for an obscene amount of time and accuse me of scamming that precious woman. I loved Nell Landry, and so did my girls. Not a day goes by that I don't think of her. Can you say the same thing?"

A muscle twitched in his jaw. Only the blinking of his eyes showed he still drew a breath. Finally he let out a long sigh.

"You know, I thought I could come out here and make a bad situation go away. I mean, I wasn't going to throw you and your daughters out on your ears today."

"Oh, really?" Sophie reluctantly paused to rein in her anger. "Exactly when did you intend to throw us out on our ears, Mr. Landry? Tomorrow, perhaps? Maybe next week?"

❧

Her question caught him off guard. That was exactly what he intended, to toss the threesome out of the house, and he had every right to do so. Why then did it sound so awful when she said it?

Because, in a way, it *was* pretty nasty.

This woman had, as far as he could tell, been a good neighbor and friend to Granny Nell. At least that was the consensus from those whose statements had been entered into evidence by the Comeaux woman's attorney.

He'd read some of the documents in the file on the flight back to the States but hadn't managed to tackle the rest of the thick packet of legal junk that still waited for him in his room.

Paperwork. He never read it. Well, rarely, anyway, until he got the packet from Calvin. In his mind, the streets of the devil's domain were covered in paperwork. Like as not, the same stuff fueled the everlasting fires down there, as well.

What he saw regarding the trial left him conflicted. If the documents didn't contain the names of people he recognized and respected, such as the pastor and two elders at church and three neighbor women, Ezra might have dismissed them. Even talkative old Miss Emmeline Trahan, the church secretary since practically the beginning of time, raved over the sweet nature of Sophie Comeaux.

And Miss Emmeline held a strong dislike for anyone but the pastor and Billy Graham.

Then there was the matter of the Mother's Day card with the note regarding orphans that virtually matched the one he'd received from Granny Nell's lawyer after she died. As much as he hated to admit it, there was a remote possibility his grandmother intended to have Sophie Comeaux and her girls as permanent houseguests. Anything beyond that, he refused to acknowledge.

Verbal sparring aside, perhaps he should give the woman a break. Maybe take a more cooperative stance, at least until he could figure a way to accomplish his mission.

He glanced back in her direction and noted the smudges of red on her cheekbones. Yep, he'd made her plenty angry.

Not that he didn't have good cause to feel the same. Still, he'd learned early on that sometimes you had to best an enemy by befriending him.

Ezra held up both hands. "Look—I'm sorry. It's obvious we both loved Nell very much. Maybe we could declare a truce. What do you say?"

Her expression turned skeptical. "A truce? Does that mean you're giving up on trying to sell my home?"

Stuffing his fists into his pockets, Ezra glanced over his shoulder. "Well, um, no."

She turned to storm inside. "Good-bye, Mr. Landry. I'll see you in court."

eleven

Ezra almost shouted a retort about looking forward to seeing *her* in court. Then he realized how very inappropriate that sort of response was. True, he wanted to win his case, complete his mission here, and get back to the real work of quietly defending his country, but perhaps the best way to beat the enemy, after all, would be to get to know him.

Or, in this case, *her*.

Not only that, but Granny Nell had raised him better than to talk like that, and the Lord kept him mindful of it all the way to his car. While the Comeaux woman had her share of apologizing to do, he knew he did, as well.

He fixed his face into a neutral expression and took a deep breath. "Buck up, Marine," he said as he straightened his posture and marched back up the walk to stare down the screen door where he'd last met the enemy.

To his surprise it swung open on loud hinges, and the woman stood in the shadows. "I owe you an apology, Mr. Landry."

She made the statement without emphasis or inflection, giving away nothing of her feelings. The juveniles appeared behind her, then scattered when she looked down to shake her head.

"I, well, um, that is. . . ." Somehow his voice quit before his thoughts were spoken. He cleared his throat. "What I mean is, Miss Comeaux, I should apologize, as well."

Another blank stare.

"Guess I should explain." He gestured to the steps. "Mind if I sit over there in the shade? I'd forgotten how hot it can get this close to October."

"The weatherman said to expect a cool spell by the end of the week."

Ezra fought the urge to mop his brow once more. "Yes, well, that would be a welcome change."

She studied him a moment longer, then shrugged. "I suppose it wouldn't hurt to sit for a minute. Just a minute though. The girls will be wanting supper soon."

He settled onto the top step and rested his elbows on his knees, then shifted positions to turn and face the front of the house. The Comeaux woman remained at the door, seemingly studying a cobweb that dangled just out of reach.

His gaze followed hers until he tired of looking up at the blue painted boards and swung his attention to the fern and then to Sophie Comeaux. His original assessment that she was the babysitter would have held even at this range. She looked entirely too youthful to be the parent of anyone.

But then what would he know of parents? His dad had bailed unofficially long before he made Ezra's arrangement with Nell official.

Nell. A pang of fresh grief hit him, and he shook it off with a roll of his shoulders. "I miss her, you know."

Only after he spoke did he realize he'd said the words out loud. His gaze jumped to the woman's face to gauge her reaction. She seemed unaffected by his rare admission of deep feelings.

Ezra turned his attention to the toes of his running shoes. While he contemplated the neatly tied laces, he tried to decide whether to be thankful or offended at the lack of attention she placed on his words. For the purpose of his current mission, he chose the former.

"I miss her, too. The girls still talk about her as if she's next door."

She'd moved from her place at the door to join him, and the fact her change in position had gone undetected worried him. One more reason to satisfy Nell's last request as quickly as possible.

"So they were close to her?" When the woman nodded, he joined her. "I shouldn't be surprised. She loved all children."

"A pity Miss Nell never had any of her own." She leaned her elbows on her knees and rested her chin in her hands. "I know she would have been a great mother. She took the girls and me on as a pet project, but I'm sure she would have preferred her own flesh and blood."

Ezra swallowed hard to try to dislodge the lump in his throat. Sadly, he failed miserably.

"Yes, I'm sure she would have," was all he could manage.

❧

Sophie cringed. "I'm so sorry. Of course she *was* a mother. She raised you, and you're her grandson, right?"

"Did she refer to me as her grandson?"

She looked a bit perplexed. "Yes, I believe she did. Why?"

Her guest's expression softened. "No reason," he said, although Sophie guessed the opposite was true.

A noise behind her alerted Sophie to the presence of the girls. She turned to see two strangely guilty faces. "What's wrong?" she asked.

The pair exchanged glances. "Nothing," Amanda said as she climbed into Sophie's lap.

"No, nothing," Chloe added, leaning against the door.

Once again she suspected she hadn't heard the full truth. Glancing down at Amanda, she thought she noticed damp eyelashes. Had her little one been crying?

Amanda met her gaze. "Mommy, why is the mean man still here?"

Shock was quickly replaced with anger. "Amanda Comeaux, you say you're sorry right now."

The younger twin turned to bury her face in Sophie's shirt as she mumbled an apology. When Sophie lifted Amanda into a sitting position and gave her a stern look, the little girl complied, although with little enthusiasm.

She was surprised when Nell's grandson shook his head. "Know what, Amanda? You're right. I haven't been very nice." He paused. "I'm very sorry. I miss my grandmother, but that's no reason to forget my manners. Besides, Granny Nell would tan my hide if she could hear how I've been acting."

Amanda drew nearer to the Landry fellow, eyes wide. "Do you know Miss Nell?"

When he nodded, Chloe inched forward. "Miss Nell's with Jesus now."

"Yes," he said, "I know." He met Sophie's gaze. "I wish I had been here."

Chloe swiped at what looked like a tear on her cheek. "She was reading her Bible when Mommy found her."

Sophie reached for her daughter. "How did you know that?"

"I heard you tell Auntie Bree." Chloe linked arms with Amanda. "We both did, didn't we, Amanda?"

Her younger sister nodded. "Yeah, and we saw the am'blance, too."

"Ambulance," Sophie corrected.

"That's what I said."

Ezra Landry stood abruptly and pressed down the creases of his jeans with the palms of his hands. He regarded Sophie with a somber look. "I wondered if maybe you would know what happened to my grandmother's Bible. I couldn't find it."

"I have it," she said, rising. "If you'll wait a moment, I'll go get it."

"No," Chloe said, jabbing Amanda. "We'll go get it, won't we, Amanda?"

"Yeah, we'll go get it," Amanda echoed.

"Do you know where it is, girls?"

"Yes, Mommy," Amanda called. "But when we were washing our hands—"

Chloe's loud shushing followed their rapid footsteps. "Never mind," the older twin called. "We know where it is."

Sophie watched the Landry fellow. He seemed to be staring at the crack over the door.

"Your grandmother did that," Sophie said. "Last Christmas."

"Oh?" He smiled. "Dare I ask?"

"It all started when the girls asked for a pink Christmas tree."

twelve

"Pink?"

Sophie shrugged. "The twins were six and had just come out of their neon-purple stage. I was thankful for that. We were nearing the one-year anniversary of their adoption. Nell and I were planning a celebration. Nothing would do, but Nell had to find a pink Christmas tree for her darlings. She always called them her darlings." Sophie paused to get hold of her emotions. "Anyway, she spread the word that she was on the lookout for a pink Christmas tree, and don't you know she found one? Someone's brother had a cousin with a tree farm or something like that."

"Sounds like Granny. She never met a stranger."

"True." Sophie looked away from his penetrating gaze to study the chipped polish on her thumbnail. Funny but until this moment, she hadn't realized the color on her nails, her favorite shade, was the same color of that memorable tree.

"So what does a pink tree have to do with cracked glass?"

"She had specified the color but forgot to specify the size. When the tree arrived, it was huge. Nine feet, at least."

Ezra's smile broadened. "What did you do, put it in the yard?"

"I considered that, but your grandmother wouldn't hear of it. The girls wanted a tree, and she intended that tree to go in the house. Nell decided the only way to get the tree to fit was to saw off the bottom. Sounded simple, except that we didn't count on wood chips flying all over. By the time she and I got that tree cut down to size, a pile of limbs sat at the curb with sawdust everywhere."

"Who did the cutting?"

"Your grandmother supervised, but the pizza delivery boy actually did the work."

"Pizza delivery boy?" He swiped at his forehead. "Where does he fit into the picture?"

"He was delivering supper to the neighbors, and Nell called him over. Next thing I know, he's cutting limbs and she's on the phone to the pizza place to explain why their delivery boy would be late."

"I'm still confused as to what this has to do with the crack over the door."

Sophie smiled. "I'm not completely sure either. All I know is when I left for work, the tree was in a bucket on the side of the house, and when I got home, it was sitting in the corner by the fireplace all decorated up with pink ribbons and silver tinsel. She never would tell me how she got it inside."

"No telling." He looked away. For a moment he seemed lost in memories of his own. "I wish I'd been here to help."

"That's the second time you've made that statement, Mr. Landry."

He looked up sharply. "Is it?"

Sophie nodded.

"Did she ever tell you why the house was split in half?"

"No." A light breeze danced across the porch, and she shivered. "I figured it was made like this."

"Oh no." Ezra crossed his arms over his chest. "When I was a kid, this was all one house. In fact, I slept in the back room."

She tucked a loose strand of hair behind her ear. "That's the kitchen now."

"Yeah, I know. I'm the one who painted those cabinets after Granddaddy and Mr. Breaux set them in place." He ran his hand over the rail. "I painted this a time or two, as well. Seems like every time I was in trouble, my punishment was to paint something. Anyway, what was the point of this story?"

"You were telling me how the house came to be split into a duplex."

The words seemed lost on her guest as he stared at the carved porch post. When he turned his attention to her, he wore what looked like a sad smile.

"It all started when Granddaddy preached a sermon on Psalm 68. What you may not know is that Granny Nell was an orphan. She was raised at the Buckner Home in Dallas after losing her mother and father to the flu epidemic in her teens."

"No," Sophie said softly, "I had no idea."

"Well, anyway, that verse about the Lord taking care of widows and the fatherless really set hard with her. She was determined to do whatever she could to make that psalm real in her life. Somehow she talked Granddaddy and Mr. Breaux into moving a wall or two inside the house. Said the three of us didn't need all that space. Anyway, I was soon painting cabinets in what used to be my bedroom."

"I'm not surprised."

He chuckled. "We had a parade of folks through that side of the house over the years. After Granddaddy passed on, something in Granny died, too. For years, 421A was empty." Nell's grandson met her gaze. "Until you."

Sophie let those last two words hang between them while she tried to decide whether their tone was accusing or merely neutral. His expression gave nothing away of his meaning, although his posture seemed unnaturally stiff. He looked like a man dealing with his past.

Maybe even a man dealing with regret.

"Here's the Bible, Mommy." Chloe emerged onto the porch and handed her the King James Bible.

"Thank you, sweetie. Now go on back inside with your sister." Sophie pressed the heavy book into Ezra's hands. "I know she loved to write in the margins. Perhaps you will find something of comfort there."

He held the Bible against his chest. "Perhaps."

A thought occurred. "Do you think that maybe the Lord sent the girls and me to make up for your absence?" When Ezra's eyes narrowed, Sophie hurried to explain. "What I mean is, your grandmother was a lady who loved to be surrounded by family. If she couldn't have you, due to the demands of your work, I mean, then maybe the Lord put the girls and me into her life to fill that void."

Ezra seemed to be considering the idea. Sophie took that as a good sign and as a signal to continue.

"Miss Nell was proud of you, Mr. Landry. She often spoke of what a valuable job you were doing for our country." Sophie waited until her guest seemed to have absorbed that statement before she made the next. "I think she understood that you would have been with her if you could have."

"Did she?"

"Well, of course," Sophie said. "You're her grandson. Why would she think otherwise?"

❧

Why indeed? Perhaps because she knew him well enough to know that his career and his dreams would never lead him back to this sleepy corner of south Louisiana. While he could claim a noble purpose in his absence, his heart told him more than patriotism was behind the career choices he'd made.

"Will you be staying at Nell's house?"

Miss Comeaux's voice commanded his attention. He focused on the crack in the glass above her head. "I hadn't considered it."

That sounded better than the full truth. What he hadn't considered was his ability to withstand the onslaught of memories, combined with the gathering shadows the evening would bring. He'd huddled for cover under enemy fire and felt less fear than the thought of spending a single night under Granny Nell's roof brought.

He'd beat it, of that Ezra was sure. Tonight, however, he'd bunk at Calvin's place.

Calvin's house was closer to the base, he told himself, and easier for everyone concerned. It was also a twenty-minute drive from Latagnier and a world away from his old life.

His stomach growled, reminding Ezra he'd passed on lunch. "I should be going," he said.

When he dared a look at Sophie Comeaux, he expected to

see relief. Instead she surprised him with a shake of her head.

"I'm sorry we got off to a bad start," she said. "Under other circumstances, we might have been. . ."

Her words tumbled into silence, but her face spoke volumes. This was not a woman used to strife. For a moment Ezra allowed himself a touch of guilt over the fact he'd brought that unwelcome element into her life.

Then he remembered his purpose, his mission. He thrust his hand in her direction. "It's been a pleasure, Miss Comeaux."

She accepted his handshake, albeit with obvious reluctance. "Welcome back to Latagnier," she said.

Ezra looked past his hostess to the pair of pint-sized females in the doorway. One wore a woman's apron tied up high under her arms. Upon closer inspection, he recognized Granny Nell's handwork on the embroidered fruit decorating the hem. He should recognize the thing. He'd ironed it enough.

"Say, that's a nice apron you've got there."

"Miss Nell gave it to us," the more bold of the two said.

"I got one, too," the other stated in a softer voice. "Want me to go get it?"

"Sure," Ezra said, although for the life of him, he couldn't say why.

What purpose did it serve to encourage conversation with the persons he would soon send packing? After all, while it might benefit him to learn more about their mother, these children wouldn't help him in his mission at all.

Perhaps he had inherited a bit of Granny Nell. Not only would she have encouraged discourse with the juveniles, why, she would probably have ended up sharing tea and cookies with them. But that was his granny.

And he was not her.

"I should go," he said.

"Wait," the girl at the door said. "Amanda's bringing her apron." She paused. "You can't leave until you see it."

Ezra glanced over at Miss Comeaux, who leaned against

the porch rail with the barest hint of a smile. He returned his attention to the apron-wearing twin.

"Of course," he said. "I'll wait."

A moment later the other twin burst through the door, slowing her pace only when she seemed to realize she'd arrived on the porch. She took one more halting step toward Ezra, then darted for the comfort of her mother's embrace.

The garment was made of handkerchiefs, each sewn together to form a checkerboard of lace and embroidery. "Do you mind if I take a closer look at that?"

The dark-haired girl peered over her shoulder. "Okay." She turned to face him, still holding her mother's hand. A second later she popped her two middle fingers in her mouth.

"I used to send Granny Nell handkerchiefs from all the places I visited." He offered the shy girl a smile. "Looks like she used them for something besides blowing her nose."

The comment brought a giggle, followed by a smile. The older twin stepped between them to join her sister. "Mommy washed it before she let Amanda wear it, so it's okay."

"Well, I'm glad about that." Ezra gave the Comeaux woman an amused look as he climbed the steps to kneel beside Amanda. Carefully he touched the corner of the garment that hung on the girl's narrow waist and puddled around her bare feet.

The detail of the tiny stitches spoke of a talent long used to create quilts and other items. The script he noticed beneath his thumb froze the breath in Ezra's lungs.

Looking closer, he realized the same handwriting appeared on most of the other squares. Only a few were void of the location and date.

"Singapore," he read. "Jakarta, Milan, Buenos Aires."

The irony of each mission to these places and the others represented on the apron was that along with the serious nature of his trips he'd always managed to make a side trip to some shop where a handkerchief might be found. Sometimes he mailed them back to Latagnier individually, while other times, when safety and national security warranted, he might send four or five in a single package.

The edge of the apron slipped from Ezra's hands as the girl shifted positions to look up at her mother. "Mommy, I'm hungry."

"You're always hungry, Amanda," the other twin said. "You just had cookies."

Both girls covered their mouths with their hands, eyes wide. Their mother's smile went south, turning into a quick frown. "Cookies?"

"Just one," Amanda said.

"Well, I just had one," the other stated, her hands on her hips. "Amanda tried to have two, but I stopped her."

"She broke the cookie jar."

"You made me."

"Maybe I can help."

The words were out before Ezra realized he'd spoken them. When three sets of female eyes stared in his direction, he knew he'd either have to elaborate or excuse himself and head for the car.

thirteen

It only took a second for Ezra to make his decision. "If I remember right, Granny Nell had a cookie jar sitting on top of her refrigerator."

"So only the grown-ups can reach it," the older twin said.

Ezra rose and straightened the crease on his jeans. "Why don't I go get the cookie jar before I leave?"

Without waiting for an answer, he bolted over to the other side of the porch and fitted the well-worn key into the lock. He was thankful it turned the first time he tried.

Ignoring the assault of memories, Ezra crossed the room to retrieve the cookie jar. The apple-shaped bin looked as if it had been freshly dusted. He turned to glance around the neat kitchen. It, too, looked as if Granny Nell had only recently performed her weekly cleaning routine.

"I try to keep things the way she left them."

Ezra looked toward the direction of the sound and found Sophie Comeaux standing in the doorway.

"It's the least I can do to honor my memory of her."

He managed a nod. Cradling the jar, he placed his hand over the stem-shaped lid and prepared to cross the minefield of his own memories. Somehow he made it, pressing past the framed pictures of his high school graduation and induction into the Marine Corps and the afghan she knitted the winter he suffered from the flu.

At the door, Ezra thrust the jar into Sophie's hands and took a step backward. An awkward silence fell between them until he caught hold of his senses and stepped toward the yard and the rental car waiting at the curb. He'd almost made it to the vehicle, keys in hand, when the childish voice called.

"Wait, Mr. Landry. You can't leave yet."

He did an about-face in the middle of the street to see the twins standing on the sidewalk. "Stay for supper," the bold one said. "On account of I want to know where the empty squares on Amanda's apron came from."

"Yeah, please," Amanda said.

What could it hurt? Just a few minutes to sit and write a couple of city names on a kid's treasured possession.

It sounded like such a harmless way to pass a half hour. He joined them for dinner, and the thirty minutes stretched to a full hour. After that came a steady diet of stories about Granny Nell, and one hour became two.

Most of the tales were told by the girls, their mother strangely silent as she went about the business of serving up grilled-cheese sandwiches and tomato soup. Ezra listened with what came close to contentment, soaking up the stories that filled the gaps since his last visit.

The girls spoke of Nell as if she were still with them, an absent neighbor rather than a woman gone on to her reward. Somehow the feeling caught hold, and before long Ezra allowed it to sink in.

He'd headed for the door with an excuse of an early wake-up call when the reality of the situation caught up with him. Tonight he'd spent one of the best evenings in recent memory with three females who would soon be homeless due to his actions. Suddenly the gift of the cookie jar didn't seem quite so magnanimous.

"Thank you for the hospitality," he said as he averted his gaze from his hostess.

The girls had finished washing the plates and were busy giggling behind the closed doors of their room. "Thank you for the jar. I'll be sure to return it to Nell's place as soon as I get a new one."

"No need," he said hastily. "I'm sure my grandmother would have wanted you to have it."

He pressed past her to step into the slightly cooler evening air. Sucking in a deep breath, he let it out slowly. Only the feeling of being watched alerted him to the fact the woman stood behind him. Steeling himself, Ezra turned to face her.

"I want you to know something, Mr. Landry." She crossed her arms over her chest and gave him the same no-nonsense look she'd given the girls before sending them to their room to prepare for bath time. "I appreciate the time you spent tonight with the girls. You were patient and kind and dealt with their questions well beyond the time when I could have handled them. You reminded the girls of Nell tonight both in your stories and in your manner. For that I am very appreciative."

Opening his mouth to respond, Ezra thought better of it and clamped his lips shut.

"But there's one thing I want you to understand. While I respect the fact that we share a deep love for Nell Landry, I must remind you that I do not share your opinion on what she intended to do with this house. In my opinion, your grandmother was crystal clear in her desire to give the girls and me a permanent home here."

Ezra whirled on his heels and strode toward the car, then threw open the door. Even from this distance, he could see the determination on the woman's face.

"We agree on one other thing, Miss Comeaux." He leaned against the roof of the car, a tight grip on his keys. "The idea of my grandmother giving you and the girls half her home is merely your opinion. But the courts rely on facts and not opinions. I am, however, willing to allow you one month in which to vacate."

"I don't need a month, sir. The answer is no."

What? Did she not realize what a generous offer he'd just made?

He decided to make one more attempt. "Miss Comeaux, if you change your mind, you can find me through my attorney. His name is on the papers you received."

"I'm all too familiar with your attorney, Major Landry. And in the future I suggest that you speak to me through my—"

"Major Landry?" Little Amanda stood beside her mother. "Do you go to our church?"

Did he? At one time he could have answered with a resounding yes. Now, well, what church did he attend? "Yes," he finally said, "I'll be there on Sunday. Why?"

She looked up at her mother before scampering down the porch steps toward him. Just short of the curb, she stopped. "Would you come home with us after church?"

"Why?" was the nicest response he could come up with.

For the answer, she came all the way toward him and wrapped her tiny hand in his. Something about the gesture made him believe this shy little girl did not befriend just anyone.

"Because me and Chloe have a present for you."

Ezra knelt to meet her eye-to-eye. "Honey, you don't have to give me a present."

"Yes, I do." Her face turned solemn. "Miss Nell said so."

"Amanda." Her mother's voice held a warning tone as she strode over to kneel beside the child. "What are you talking about?"

"Mommy, I can't tell you *now*." She looked up at Ezra, then back at Sophie. "Miss Nell made me promise it was a surprise—only Chloe and me kinda spilled water on it so now it has to dry."

"Spilled it on what?"

"On the *secret*."

Ezra nodded as if he understood, which he didn't. But then he'd never been one to contemplate the complexities of the female mind for long. He found it left him with a headache.

Sophie Comeaux gave him a look that would freeze hot cider. A second later she managed a sweet smile in her daughter's direction. "Well, sweetheart, Mr. Landry is a busy man. Can we bring the secret to church and give it to him there?"

The girl seemed to consider the idea for a moment. "I suppose so." Reluctance showed on Amanda's face and couldn't be missed in her voice. "But do we hafta? I like him." She glanced in his direction and offered Ezra a gap-toothed smile. "He's funny like Miss Nell."

Sophie stood to offer Ezra a frustrated look. "I suppose we will see you on Sunday then. I usually park behind the choir entrance, so let's meet there after services."

It didn't take an expert to know this female was not thrilled with the idea of seeing him again. Maybe he'd make it easy on the kid and tell her mama he'd accept whatever she had for him by mail. Better yet, through his attorney.

He intended to say just that. Somehow, though, when he looked down into the little girl's wide brown eyes, he heard himself say, "See you Sunday then."

fourteen

October 2

With the girls' soccer practice going on nearby, Sophie leaned back against the park bench and held up her thumb and forefinger. "I tell you, Bree—I felt this big."

"Why?"

"I mean, we talk about turning the other cheek and heaping burning coals on the enemy's head with our kindnesses, and I tried. But when I looked at the man who is trying to take my home away from me, I. . ." She paused to take a deep breath. "I'm ashamed to say I didn't handle the situation very well."

She studied the box on the bench between them. A dozen juice boxes and a container of orange slices made for a colorful display, one the soccer players would demolish once their practice ended.

"You fed the man, Soph. I don't know if I would have let him in the house." Bree rubbed her hands over her arms and shivered. "What time is it?"

Sophie checked her watch. "Quarter to ten. Why?"

Bree groaned. "How do you do it? It's Saturday morning and freezing cold. Why can't your girls watch cartoons until noon like proper young ladies?" When Sophie frowned, Bree held up her hands. "I'm only kidding. Auntie Bree is thrilled to go with you to soccer practice. I love those girls. Still, wasn't it like a hundred degrees yesterday?"

She glanced over at Bree's lime green nylon jogging suit and matching sneakers with fur-trimmed socks, an outfit more at home in the mall than out at the soccer fields. A half-dozen silver bangles, designer sunglasses, and a pair of stylish pearl earrings completed the ensemble. Beneath the thin jacket, a white T-shirt was emblazoned with JOG written in green glitter.

In comparison, Sophie's Audubon Zoo sweatshirt, faded jeans, and well-worn running shoes were warm and comfortable. Like as not, Bree would be calling for cold meds before sundown. In the meantime, though, her friend looked fabulous.

"We had a blue norther, Bree, which you would have heard about had you been watching the news instead of the fashion channel." Sophie followed Bree's gaze and chuckled. "And as for coming to watch the girls, I'm thinking you wouldn't mind going out with their coach either."

"Point number one, I don't watch the fashion channel, dear. I make fashion, not follow it. You ought to know that by now." She offered a broad smile and a flick of her wrist. The bangles jingled as they caught the light.

"Yes, you've got me there. I will concede that point, Counselor. Now, about the coach?"

Bree cast a glance over to where the lone adult male on the field was putting ten girls through dribbling practice. "I barely noticed that handsome, single, godly deputy sheriff who always sits in front of me at Sunday services. I only have eyes for the girls." She pointed to the field where Amanda and Chloe were racing along with the other girls. "Speaking of the twins, how did they handle your visitor? Did they know who he was?"

"Yes, they knew," she said. "And they were great." Sophie sighed. "In fact, Amanda asked him to come back on Sunday."

Bree leaned back and shook her head. "He's coming back to your house? You're kidding?"

"I didn't say he was *coming*. I said Amanda *invited* him. I told him where I parked my car and said we would meet him after church." At Bree's confused look, she continued. "The girls have a gift for him. Something Nell wanted him to have." Sophie sighed. "When I asked what that was, the girls said it was a secret. Honestly, I don't like it, but I have to let them do this. It seems to be really important to them."

"A gift?" She shook her head. "For the man who's trying to kick you and the girls to the curb? Oh, I have a *gift* for him all right." Bree met her stare. "Seriously, Soph. What was he like? I'm asking as your attorney now, not just as your friend."

"He was. . . What do I say to describe a man bent on sending me out on my ear?"

"Forget character sketches, Soph. Tell me your impression of the man. Was he sleazy, nice, mean, sneaky, what?"

"He was nice to the girls, and I suppose one could argue he was nice to me. After all, he did offer me a great deal."

"Yeah," Bree said. "A month's free rent before eviction. Gotcha. What else do you recall about him?"

A chill wind slithered past, and Sophie suppressed a shiver. "I don't know, Bree. Does it matter?"

"It matters." Bree touched her arm. "Ideally I would like to get a feeling for what he's like. I want to know what he thinks, what he believes, and anything else that will give me insight into what his side might throw at us in trial."

Sophie tucked a strand of hair behind her ear. "Like what?"

"Well, like what is his level of commitment to this action? If Ezra Landry is a reasonable man, maybe he can come to understand that his grandmother wanted you and the girls to have the house. I emphasize the word *maybe*."

"Can't you just explain it to him? You knew Nell almost as well as I did, and you're a lawyer. He might listen to you."

"I can't do that. Ezra Landry has legal representation; thus I am enjoined from communication outside those channels."

Sophie raised her brows, and Bree added, "Legally I can only speak to his attorney, not him."

"Oh."

The coach's whistle chirped, signaling the end of practice. In response the girls raced to huddle in a circle around him.

Sophie sighed. A few minutes from now, ten girls would come running toward them wanting juice boxes and orange slices. She'd hoped a conversation with Bree might lead her to a solution. Now that their time together had almost run out, she was nowhere near solving the conundrum that Ezra Landry's lawsuit had become.

Then an idea dawned. "But I'm not enjoined, am I? From talking to Ezra, I mean."

"Oh, I don't like the sound of this already, and I don't even know what you're planning." Bree gave her a sideways look. "Do you even know what *enjoined* means?"

"Yes, madam attorney, I know what *enjoined* means. What I want to know is, are there any laws against me speaking to the man?"

"In general, no." She leaned forward. "In specific, maybe. What do you have in mind?"

Sophie smiled. "Don't worry, Bree. I'm not going to do anything stupid."

"Define *stupid*," Bree said as the girls came rushing up. "In my opinion, spending any amount of time with the opposing party in a lawsuit is the opposite of smart." She spied the deputy heading in their direction and pasted on a broad smile before leaning over to address Sophie. "And in case you're not catching my meaning, the opposite of smart is stupid. Just stay away from him and let the professionals handle this."

Reaching for the bowl of orange slices, she shook her head. "Don't worry, Bree. I'm only trying to make this lawsuit go away so the girls and I can live in peace." She chuckled. "I'm not going to fall in love with him or anything."

"Who's in love?"

Bree looked past her. "Well, hello there, Deputy. Speaking of love, I just love those sunglasses of yours. You must tell me where you found them. I need to buy my brother a birthday gift, and that's exactly what I'm looking for."

For the next few minutes, Bree and the girls' coach carried on a conversation about everything from sunglasses and the weather to the color green and the health benefits of jogging. Through it all, Sophie handed out juice boxes and orange slices while marveling at her friend's easy and enviable ability to speak to men. Before the last girl left, Bree had secured a date for a jog at the park that afternoon.

"Despite what your T-shirt says, you don't jog, Bree," Sophie said when the coach left. "And guess what? I happen to know Phil is a marathon runner. How are you going to keep up?"

Bree grinned. "That is the least of my worries." She rose and gathered her purse and keys. "The real concern is what will I wear?"

"Bree!"

"I'm kidding." She shook her head. "Hey, girls, how about we celebrate your win with pancakes?"

Chloe giggled. "Nobody won, Auntie Bree. This was a *practice*."

"Just a practice, eh? Well, I guess that means no one wants pancakes, since it was just a *practice*. And, of course, no one would want to ride with the *top* down over to the diner on this glorious day."

A pair of seven-year-old voices rose in disagreement. Sophie covered her mouth with her hand so the girls wouldn't see her amusement.

"Well now," Bree said as she tapped her temple with her forefinger. "Help me out here? Do we have a consensus? A ride in my convertible followed by pancakes at the Magnolia Café." When the girls squealed their approval, Bree held up her hands to silence them. "Shall we invite your mom?"

Three sets of eyes turned in Sophie's direction. "You guys go on and save me a place. I'll be right there. I just have a quick call to make."

Bree clicked the alarm on her car, then pushed the button to set the top in motion. The girls raced across the grass, each claiming the front seat as they ran.

"Backseat, both of you, and buckle up," Bree called. "You know the rules. Oh, and cover up with that blanket I left on the floor."

"You have a blanket?" Sophie chuckled. "Why didn't you get it out when you were so cold back there on the bench?"

"It didn't match." She stood shoulder to shoulder with Sophie until the girls were settled in the car; then she turned to face her friend, a serious look on her face. "Soph? What are you planning?"

"Nothing my lawyer would disapprove of," she said.

Bree's eyes narrowed. "Why do I doubt you?"

"Oh, ye of little faith," she said with a giggle as she tossed the remains of the morning snack into a bag.

"Oh, me who knows you too well." Bree shook her head. "Promise me you won't do anything to jeopardize this case."

She looked her friend in the eye. "I promise. Remember what I have to lose here."

"All right, then." Bree shouldered her handbag and followed Sophie toward the parking lot.

Sophie tossed the bag into the trash container at the edge of the parking lot, then strolled over to kiss the girls. "Be right there, I promise," she said.

Once Bree's convertible disappeared around the corner, Sophie climbed into her van and shut the door. In contrast to the chilly weather outside, the sun had warmed the vehicle's interior to a toasty temperature. For a moment she wished for Bree's lighter-weight ensemble.

She riffled through her purse until she found the business card she'd tossed in there more than a month ago. Setting the card on the console, she reached for her cell phone and punched in the numbers. Expecting to leave a message, she jumped when she heard a man's voice on the line.

"Mr. Dubose, please."

"This is Major Dubose."

Major. Sophie suppressed a groan. In the background she heard noises that indicated he might be outdoors.

"I'm terribly sorry to bother you on a Saturday, but. . ." She paused in an attempt to collect her thoughts and exit the call gracefully. "I was trying to get in touch with Ezra Landry. I know he's a client of yours. I can call back and leave a message on voice mail if you'd like."

fifteen

"No, really, it's fine," Ezra heard Calvin say. "I'm afraid I'm at a little disadvantage though. You see, I'm not in my office."

Ezra continued to loosen the lug nut on the spare tire while his buddy made himself comfortable leaning against the lone tree in the narrow front yard of Calvin's on-base house. The task complete, Ezra moved on to the next and found it wouldn't budge.

"Hey, Cal, you gonna talk all day, or are you going to help me get this car back on the road?" When Calvin smiled and waved away the question, Ezra's irritation rose. "Look, pal—this is your car, and I'm doing all the work."

"Yes," Calvin said to the caller, "in fact, that is Mr. Landry. Would you like to speak to him?"

He held the phone out to Ezra, chuckling. "It's for you. Now give me that lug wrench, and I'll show you what a real soldier can do."

"Who is it?"

Calvin mouthed the words, "A woman."

Ezra took the phone and watched Calvin strut back to the car, laughing all the way. "What's so funny?" he called, but Calvin merely pointed to the phone. "Hello?" he finally said. "Landry here."

"Mr. Landry? This is Sophie Comeaux."

He shot a look at Calvin that would scald a cat. Did Calvin know to whom he was speaking? Surely not. The look his buddy gave him was full of too much amusement to know the caller was the interloper now occupying Nell Landry's house.

"Hello? Are you there?"

Returning his attention to the phone, Ezra offered Calvin

82

his back. No way could he concentrate with Cal staring at him. "Yes, I'm here."

"I'm sure you're surprised to hear from me."

Ezra left the statement hanging between them. He had nothing he wanted to say to her, nor did he intend to encourage any sort of conversation. If he remained silent, perhaps she would hang up more quickly.

"I remembered that you said if I wanted to speak to you I should contact you through your lawyer."

Silence. If she were here, he'd give her the boot camp look. That usually had one of two effects: gleaning the truth or sending the party running. In this case he'd vote for the running.

"I was just at the park, and, well, I guess you're not interested in why I was at the park."

"Nope."

"Yes, well, all right," she said. "Anyway, I found Mr. Dubose's—"

"Major Dubose."

"Yes, um, Major Dubose. Anyway, I found his card and figured I would leave a message, but instead he answered."

"You should have. Left a message, I mean."

"I couldn't. He answered."

A carpenter ant made its way up the porch post, and Ezra studied it. As it reached the flat surface of the rail, Ezra flicked it onto the ground where it reconnoitered and began its climb once more. When it reached the rail, he sent it flying again, only to watch it head for the post one more time.

Like that ant, Ezra felt he was getting nowhere fast.

"Is this about the house, Miss Comeaux? Because if you're accepting my offer, you could've told Calvin instead of me."

"The house?" Sophie paused, and Ezra hoped she was trying to figure out how to tell him she'd given up the fight. "I suppose it is about the house," she continued. "Sort of."

"Then I need to give the phone back to the major."

"Look—I know you had plans to meet the girls after church tomorrow, but I was wondering. . . ." She paused. "I was wondering if instead you might be willing to come to a barbecue at my house a week from today."

My house. It took all he had not to correct her on that.

She continued without waiting for his answer. "I know it's a bit chilly out today, but the weatherman says we should be warming up tomorrow. Temperatures should be back in the 70s by next week. Perfect weather for a barbecue. You can come Saturday at five, can't you?"

"Five?" He turned to look at Calvin for help but found the man's legs sticking out from under the car. Evidently he'd decided the lug nuts weren't a priority.

Great.

"Is that too early?"

Ezra forced his attention back to the conversation. "Early? No, it's fine, but. . ."

But what? He could probably find a million excuses for not attending this thing, but what if she intended to tell him in person that she was taking his offer?

"But you're probably wondering why I would invite you to dinner, considering."

"Yeah," he said. "Considering."

"Two reasons." She paused. "First off, I'm not proud of how I reacted to the current situation. And, second, I wonder if. . . I sort of hoped that once you get to know the girls and me, you will see what Nell meant to us."

At the mention of his grandmother, all the nice went out of the conversation. "I'm busy Saturday," he said. "Thanks anyway."

"Give us a chance, Ezra. What if you're wrong about your grandmother's wishes?"

He wanted to say no, wanted it with everything he had. Strange, but he opened his mouth, and the opposite sentiment came out. "Would you mind if I brought Calvin along?"

"Your lawyer?"

Her surprise stumped him. If she intended to give up, wouldn't she want to finalize matters as quickly as possible?

He understood a lot of things, but women were not one of them. "Is that a no?" he fired back.

"No. I mean, that's fine. I suppose."

"So it's a yes?"

Another pause and what sounded like a sigh. "Yes," Sophie said slowly, "I suppose it is."

Ezra closed the fancy phone and set it on the porch rail in the path of the carpenter ant. This time he let the insect make its way around the obstacle to continue on.

Reaching for the lug wrench, Ezra strolled to the car and tapped the bumper. Hard.

Calvin shot out from under the car with a scowl. "What did you do that for?" he asked, rubbing his head.

"Cancel your plans for next Saturday night." Ezra knelt to tackle the stubborn lug nut with renewed fervor.

"I don't have plans for next Saturday night."

He smiled as the metal gave way and the lug loosened. "You do now, my friend. We're going to a barbecue."

❧

"A barbecue?" Bree shook her head. "Oh no, I don't think so. This is highly irregular."

Sophie leaned forward and rested her elbows on the table. She was glad the girls had met up with friends from the soccer team and were now headed for an afternoon playdate. The unplanned afternoon alone would be wonderful; the unplanned conversation with her attorney, though, less so.

"Irregular but not illegal, right?"

Bree considered the question a moment, then shot back several of her own in response. Once Sophie had answered them all to Bree's satisfaction, the attorney nodded.

"All right, I will give my blessing to this." Bree met Sophie's gaze. "But I don't want you to sign anything, you hear? Nothing. Not even a paper napkin."

Nodding, Sophie picked up her purse and reached for the

check. "Oh, don't worry. You'll be there to keep me from making any mistakes."

"I'll what?" Bree rose to follow Sophie to the cashier. "Oh no, you don't. I am *not* going to put my official stamp of approval on this by actually attending."

"But you said it would be okay."

Slipping a twenty to the cashier, Bree frowned. "I said I would give this harebrained scheme of yours my *blessing*. That's off the record, Soph, and only because I have seen some room for compromise in his case. I can't just show up there. Opposing counsel will think it's a setup. Besides, I have a lunch meeting next Saturday with a client."

"Then there's no problem." Sophie replaced Bree's twenty with her own, then handed the money to the cashier. "You don't have to be at my place until five." She tucked Bree's money into her friend's purse, then offered her a broad smile. "See how nicely that works out?"

"Nice?" Bree shook her head. "I have a bad feeling about this, Soph. Tell me you'll reconsider."

Sophie affected a thinking pose by placing her knuckles against her forehead. A second later she dropped her hand to her waist and smiled. "Okay, I thought about it. Be there at four thirty."

"I thought you said five."

Turning on her heels, Sophie headed for the door. "I did, but I forgot how well you can toss a salad." She stopped at the curb to face Bree. "You'll be there, won't you? Please?"

"Hey, Bree, ready for our run?"

Sophie grasped Bree's arm as the girls' soccer coach jogged toward them. "Bree, you just ate Belgian waffles. How do you propose to run?"

Her friend offered a grin that broadened into a wide smile as her date drew near. "Well, hello there, Deputy," she said. "You're just in time."

He sent an acknowledging wave toward Sophie, then turned his attention to Bree. "I am?"

"Yes, you are." Bree gave Sophie a sideways look, then reached out to touch the coach's arm. "I know we were supposed to go jogging, but I was wondering—would you happen to be any good with cars?"

"Cars?" The big guy took the bait in two seconds flat. "Sure," he said with an air of authority. "What seems to be the trouble?"

Bree winked at Sophie, then strolled toward her convertible. "It's kind of hard to explain. Maybe I could take you for a ride and show you." She paused. "Unless you'd rather run."

The next thing Sophie knew, she was waving at Bree and the soccer coach as they sped down the road. "If only I had a way with men like she does," Sophie muttered as she climbed into the van.

As soon as the words were out, she groaned. The last thing she needed to cultivate was the skill of attracting men. She'd already attracted one too many.

A memory threatened, and with practiced skill she pushed it away. Her hand shaking, she attempted to fit the key into the ignition, only to watch it fall to the floor.

Hot tears threatened. "This is silly," she muttered as she leaned down to retrieve the keys.

"What's silly, *chere*?" a feminine voice called. "And tell me quick because I've got the best news."

sixteen

"Call her back." Calvin swiped at the grease on his forehead, only making the stain worse. "I'm telling you, this can only spell bad news."

"Are you serious?" Ezra let the wrench drop into the tool box, then knelt beside the car to check his work on the lug nuts. "What am I supposed to do? Tell her my lawyer won't let me go?"

"Yes."

"Yes?" He watched Calvin stand and dust off his jeans, then head for the house. "And if you don't, I will," he said over his shoulder.

"Wait a minute." Ezra fell in step beside his friend. "I've been handling my own dating calendar for years, Cal. I don't need you to speak to a woman for me."

Calvin stopped and gave him an odd look. "What did you say?"

"What?" He searched his mind for anything that might have caused Calvin to react so strongly. Nothing.

"You said it was a date."

Ezra shook his head. "Oh, come on. I didn't say that. Well, maybe I used that word, but you know what I meant."

"Do I?" Calvin reached for the door knob, then turned back to face Ezra. "I'm very worried about this situation, Ezra. I am concerned you may be getting a little too close to the opposing party here."

Indignation rose, and he pressed past Calvin to step inside. "I am not," he said as he tossed his keys and wallet onto the counter. "In fact, my plan is to get to know the woman a bit better so I can help you do your job."

Calvin chuckled. "Did I ask for help?"

"No, but I—"

"But nothing, my friend. I don't want you anywhere near that house until the court declares it yours. Got it?"

"Are you serious? That's *my* house."

"A woman and two children are in that house, and neither of you is arguing the point that she is there at your grandmother's invitation. The courts are not in the habit of forcing people out when they've been invited in."

Ezra took a step backward and shook his head. "Hey, wait a minute. Are you saying I don't have a case?"

His buddy hit the hot water faucet with his elbow, then reached for the soap before looking up. "What I'm saying is, given the circumstances and the current leanings of the court, I think you can win this. Just don't make my job any harder."

Calvin immersed his greasy hands in the stream of water and began scrubbing while Ezra sighed. How had the situation become so complicated? One moment he had a perfectly good reason to strongly dislike the interlopers residing in his house. Then, in a matter of hours, those same interlopers had taken him in, fed him, and invited him back for a barbecue.

To make matters worse, the two girls promised to give him a present. No one besides Granny Nell had given him a present in years. Much as he hated to admit it, the thought of a gift made him smile. After all, their mother was the perpetrator of the fraud, not Chloe and Amanda. The girls were innocent in all this.

A gift. *I wonder what it is.*

"Oh, tell me I'm not seeing this."

Ezra glanced up to see his friend staring. The expression on his face showed disgust.

"What?"

"That look." Calvin threw the kitchen towel onto the counter, never breaking eye contact. "My friend, you look positively, well, attached."

"What does that mean?"

Calvin walked past him without comment and headed

down the hall to the spare bedroom where Ezra bunked. He emerged with a file in his hand, the file he'd given Ezra concerning the lawsuit against Sophie Comeaux. The marine attorney stopped at the kitchen where he tossed the file onto the table. He then reached beneath the sink to retrieve the wastebasket. Only then did Calvin look up at Ezra.

"What are you doing?" Ezra leaned against the counter and shook his head. "Are you trying to make a point, because I'm missing it completely?"

In the place of his normal expression, Calvin wore the look of a full-combat marine. "Choose," echoed in the kitchen.

Ezra chuckled. "What are you talking about?"

"Either you are going to be my client, or you are going to be that woman's dinner guest. Choose."

"Oh, come on, Cal. It's a harmless barbecue. What can happen?" When no answer seemed forthcoming, Ezra tried another tack. "Look—her girls have a gift for me from my grandmother. They're just kids, innocent in all this. I don't want to hurt their feelings by not showing up."

"But wasn't the original plan that you would meet them after church tomorrow?" He reached for the file, then clutched it to his chest and waited for an answer.

"Well, yes."

"So let me get this straight." Calvin's eyes narrowed. "If you're willing to sip tea with them and attend social events together, why are you so intent on kicking them out of your house?"

"Because it's the right thing to do." He let out a long breath. "Because I need to do this for Granny Nell."

"And you're 100 percent sure this is what your grandmother wanted? While we're on the subject, are you sure this is what God is telling you to do?"

Was he? Ezra's brain screamed a *yes* while his heart. . .his heart told him he might not have given the matter as much thought and prayer as he should have.

"That's what I thought." Calvin stuffed the file into the

wastebasket, then shoved the container back under the sink.

Before Ezra could find his voice, his friend and attorney had disappeared into the bathroom. The sound of running water announced he was headed for the shower.

For a moment Ezra stood in the hall. Just stood. The rightness of his case for following his attorney's advice contrasted sharply with the churning in his gut.

Granny Nell always said a man knew when the Lord was trying to tell him something. Could this be one of those times?

Ezra leaned against the bathroom door and stared up at the ceiling. Eyes closed, he began to search his heart. It only took a moment to decide he didn't like what he found there.

ߪ

"Miss Emmeline." Sophie straightened and took a deep breath, letting it out slowly as her heart slowed its racing. Placing both hands on the wheel, she said, "I didn't see you there."

The grande dame of Latagnier wore denim today in the form of a tasteful if not dated pantsuit and matching pumps. She carried a purse that resembled a leopard-print bowling bag. A leopard-trimmed broach on her collar completed the outfit. In all, the outfit was rather subdued for the flamboyant church secretary and president of the historical society.

"Oh, I frightened you." Emmeline Trahan rested her perfectly polished red nails on the car door and affected a mock pout. "Will you forgive me? I was just so excited about my news that I spoke before I thought."

"Of course," Sophie said. "So what's this about some news?"

"Oh, it's just wonderful. I'm so excited." She clapped her hands, and her rings caught the light, reflecting a rainbow of colors into the van. "I wonder if I could buy you a cup of coffee. That is, if you aren't busy with the girls." Miss Emmeline stuck her head inside the van window. "Looks like you're all alone."

"Chloe and Amanda are with friends for a few hours."

Miss Emmeline gave her a satisfied smile. "Then we have loads of time. Come—let's talk inside."

Somehow Sophie found herself back in the Magnolia Café before she could protest. Not that anyone had much luck changing the spry septuagenarian's mind once it had been made up.

Settling into a booth by the front window, Miss Emmeline offered a smile to the waiter. "How're your mama and daddy, Ernie?" Before the young man could answer, Miss Emmeline reached over to grab Sophie's hand. "Do you know who this young fellow is?"

Sophie looked up at the boy whose attention seemed to be fixed on the ceiling. "I'm sorry. I don't."

"This is Ernest Breaux III." At the sound of the name, the young man flinched. "Isn't that right?"

"Yes, ma'am," he said softly.

Miss Emmeline smiled. "Ernie's great-grandpapa was one of our founding fathers and a right nice man, as I hear tell. Theophile Breaux was his name. Ernest Sr., Theo's eldest son and Ernie's grandfather, married one of the Lamonts. He turned out the best quality furniture in the state from his workshop down by Bayou Nouvelle. Ernie's kin to our esteemed cardiologist Dr. Villare, Mr. Arceneaux at the Dip Cone, as well as a host of others in this area including me. Isn't that right, young man?"

The teenager studied his pencil and nodded. "Yes, ma'am," he mumbled without interest. "I guess."

"You guess?" Miss Emmeline straightened her spine and gripped the edge of the table with both hands. "My dear boy, you are the scion of a grand family, as am I." She regarded Sophie with a solemn look. "I'm kin to Theo's wife. Clothilde was a Trahan before she married. She was my cousin," she said before returning her attention to Ernie. "Our people settled this area. Without them, Latagnier might never have become the fair city it now is."

He stared at Miss Emmeline, clearly unimpressed. "Did

you want anything besides coffee?"

"Two menus and a smile, please." When she realized Ernie had missed the joke, she waved her hand to dismiss him. "Just the menus then."

Sophie watched the young man shuffle away, his baggy pants and overlong shirttail not marking him as anything other than a typical teen. "I wonder if he understands what a wonderful gift a family history is."

"Oh, I don't know, *chere*," Miss Emmeline said, "I doubt young people care much for anything in the past. He might someday, though."

"It's all so interesting, this connection with history. I grew up in the city where we didn't even know our neighbors."

"What a pity, dear," Miss Emmeline said. "Must make a body feel like she's drifting without an anchor, eh?"

Drifting without an anchor. What an apt description of her life before Nell Landry.

Ernie returned with the menus and his notepad. "Ready?"

"Coffee, please," Sophie said.

He turned to Miss Emmeline. "Ma'am?"

"I think we can change this lack of understanding about our past," Miss Emmeline said. "In fact, that's what I wanted to talk to you about, Sophie. Our founding fathers' celebration, that is." She returned her attention to poor Ernie as if she'd just noticed he stood nearby. "We'd like two cups of café au lait and a plate of beignets, please."

"Just black coffee for me," Sophie hastened to add as Ernie headed for the kitchen. "Now what were you saying about a founding fathers' celebration?"

"It's all very last minute, but then sometimes the best things are, eh?" Miss Emmeline heaved a sigh. "I've got the go-ahead from the powers that be to put on a festival next month, the sixteenth."

"What does that have to do with me?"

"Oh, plenty." She reached over to touch Sophie's hand. "I'm counting on you to help me with an important project. I have decided that a founders' celebration would be incomplete without a celebration of our founders, eh?"

Sophie nodded.

"Since this is our first-ever festival, our theme will encompass the founding families and their contribution to Latagnier. At the same time I feel it's important to acknowledge a hometown hero or heroine, as well. Someone who embodies the spirit of Latagnier."

"I agree," Sophie said. "But I still don't see how I can help with this. Are you asking me to choose someone to honor?"

Ernie returned with two coffees and a plate of beignets. Miss Emmeline waited until he left to respond.

"Oh no, dear. We have an honoree already chosen. What I need from you is help putting together the presentation to honor her." The church secretary took a healthy bite of beignet, dusting the table and her lap with powdered sugar. "I do love our little fried donuts. Are you sure you won't have one?" She pressed the plate toward Sophie.

She took a sip of coffee, then set the cup down. "Dear girl, I'm talking in circles, aren't I? The recipient of the founders' award is going to be Nell Landry, the late Reverend Landry's wife."

"Oh, that's wonderful. Nell was such a dear woman, and she did so much for Latagnier."

"I agree. We'd like to have a plaque made to hang in city hall along with the founders' portraits. And since you and she were so close, it's only natural you should be the one to put together the presentation. Something simple and reverent to honor a godly woman."

"Presentation?" Sophie reached for the spoon and gave her coffee a stir. "Miss Emmeline, I'm a nurse. I wouldn't know the first thing about putting a presentation together. Besides, I work full-time. Then there're the girls. . . ."

"Oh dear." The church secretary fretted with her napkin; then a smile dawned. "Well, of course. Why didn't I think of it sooner? I brought a list of people who might be good sources of stories about Nell, folks who knew her way back when. That ought to get you started."

Sophie reached for the paper Miss Emmeline handed her, then scanned the page. Several dozen names and phone numbers were followed by notes like "knew her in childhood" or "worked for Pastor Landry."

"I know this is a surprise and there's little time to work on it," Miss Emmeline said. "If I found someone to work with you on this, would you feel more comfortable accepting the responsibility of completing it?"

Sophie considered the question a moment before nodding. "I suppose. As long as I don't have to do any public speaking."

"I promise. You do the work, and I'll assign the talking to your partner. The one I have in mind will surely agree to that." She swung her gaze to meet Sophie's stare. "Now when will you be available to begin?"

seventeen

"Hurry up, Amanda. We need to get this finished before Mommy comes to turn out the lights."

Sophie stood at the door to her daughters' room, a stack of photo albums resting in the crook of her arm. She'd begun the daunting project of capturing the essence of Nell Landry as soon as she returned from picking up the girls.

Looking through photographs from the last two years seemed the place to start. She had retrieved the albums from her closet and set them on the kitchen table, only to find that she couldn't manage to look at more than two or three pictures of Nell without crying. The albums had been moved to the coffee table where they sat all through dinner and the kiddie movie she watched with the girls.

Now, with bedtime looming, she decided to take the albums into her room. The story of Nell would become her bedtime story. Or at least that was the theory.

"Girls, what are you doing in there?"

"Nothing," Chloe quickly responded.

"Coloring," Amanda added.

Sophie moved past the door to deposit the photo albums on her bed, then returned to listen in on a heated conversation between Chloe and Amanda regarding whether or not to tell their mother about the work they still needed to do. While Chloe favored doing the work, whatever it was, under the sheets with the flashlight, Amanda suggested asking for permission to stay up later.

Having heard enough, Sophie stepped into the doorway and leaned on the frame, crossing her hands over her chest. "Ready for bed, girls?"

Amanda regarded her with wide eyes while Chloe stuffed

something under her pillow, then affected an angelic expression. Neither spoke.

"You're not even in your pajamas yet," Sophie said. "What's going on here? I sent you to brush your teeth and get ready for bed half an hour ago."

"We were really busy, Mommy," Amanda said, her eyes downcast. "We need to finish something."

Chloe gave Amanda a shove. "Tattletale."

"Chloe," Sophie said sharply. "Apologize this very minute."

Her mumbled "I'm sorry" failed to carry much enthusiasm. Easygoing Amanda, however, accepted it without reservation and responded by hugging her sister and saying she was sorry, too.

Sophie picked her way past the crayons and markers scattered on the pink rug that covered the old wood floor. Gathering the twins into her arms, she settled onto Chloe's bed.

"Girls, is there anything you'd like to tell me?" When neither responded, she turned her attention to the older and more outspoken of the two. "Why don't you start, Chloe?"

The little girl quickly looked away. It was obvious she wasn't ready to spill the beans.

She turned her attention to Amanda. "Anything you want to tell me, missy?"

Amanda exchanged a serious glance with her sister. For a second it seemed as though she might confess.

"No, Mommy, there's nothing." She paused to toy with the hem of her shirt. " 'Sides, I can't tell you. It's a secret."

Chloe squirmed at her side. "That's right," she said slowly. "If we tell you, then it will give away the secret."

Sophie set the girls side by side on the bed, then rose to kneel at eye level to them. She covered Chloe's fingers with her right hand and Amanda's with her left. Of the pair, Chloe wore the more worried expression.

"What's wrong, sweetheart?" she asked Chloe.

Dark eyes shut tight, then blinked hard before opening to stare in her direction. A conflict of some sort played across her daughter's face. In a flash her confused expression turned to a pleading look.

"It's not a bad secret, Mommy. I promise."

Amanda squeezed her hand. "That's right. It's not bad. I promise, too."

"Girls, what do I say about making promises?"

"Never make a promise unless you intend to keep it," they said in unison.

"That's right." She paused to consider her next question. "And secrets," she said slowly. "What's the rule about keeping secrets from Mommy?"

"No secrets," Amanda said, "unless it's a present."

"That's right." Sophie lifted her girls' hands to her lips and kissed them both, then held them against her heart. "This secret of yours, is it a present?"

"Oh yes, Mommy," Chloe said. "That's why we can't tell."

"We promised Miss Nell." Amanda covered her mouth. "Oops."

"Amanda!" Chloe frowned at her sister. "You're such a blabbermouth."

"I am not."

"Are, too."

Sophie released the girls and stood. "All right now. That's enough. Chloe, if I have to remind you again of the proper way to treat your sister, you will not be going home with Heather after school on Monday. And as for you," she said to Amanda, "please think about whether or not what you tell me will give away the good secret, okay?"

"I'll try, Mommy," Amanda said.

"So are we straight on secrets and promises?" When they nodded, she tapped her temple. "Remind me, girls. What happens in the morning?"

"Church," Amanda said.

"And Sunday school," Chloe added.

"That's right. And what time do we go to bed the night before church and Sunday school?"

"Nine o'clock," they said together.

"Very good." Sophie knelt to grab a handful of crayons and toss them into the bin. "Now anyone care to tell me what time it is?"

"Eight forty-five," Chloe said.

"Fifteen minutes until bedtime and you two haven't changed into your pajamas or brushed your teeth. Guess you must not want a story tonight."

"But, Mommy, the part with the lion was just getting good. We have to find out what happens next," Amanda said.

"Then scoot, both of you," Sophie replied. "If you can brush and change quickly enough, you just might have time."

The words were barely out of her mouth before the girls, pajamas in hand, raced from the room toward the bathroom. Sophie listened to their chatter while she picked up the rest of the mess left on the rug. Any other time she would have made the girls do the cleaning up, but tonight she relished the simple task.

The job complete, she set the bin back on the shelf. The water came on in the bathroom, indicating that the girls had begun to brush their teeth. In a moment they would come rushing back in to climb under the covers. A story would surely follow, even though the clock ticked dangerously toward nine.

An extra few minutes to finish the chapter wouldn't hurt. Besides, that gave her a few more minutes to avoid the task of looking through the photographs.

She turned back Amanda's lacy pink quilt and plumped up her pillow, then moved to Chloe's bed to do the same. So alike and yet so different, Chloe's bedcovers, a pattern of pastel squiggles and polka dots against a pink satin top, were uniquely her.

When she lifted the covers, she saw something half hidden between the mattress and the wall. It was dark and—

"Mommy, we're ready," Amanda called.

Sophie replaced the pillow and took her spot in the rocker

near the window. Reaching for the book, she watched the door as the girls filed in.

"Ready for the rest of the chapter?" she asked.

Not only did she finish that chapter, but she read well into the next. Only the girls' yawns caused her to close the book and kiss them good night.

When she returned to her room, the pile of photo albums greeted her. So did the memories.

"Maybe I'll tackle this tomorrow," she whispered as she lifted the stack of albums off the bed and cradled them in her arms. "Or Monday after work. Yep, that's probably best."

But as she stacked them neatly on the bedside table, she knew there would never be a good day to confront the loss of Nell Landry.

eighteen

October 3

Ezra stepped into the late-morning sunshine and inhaled deeply of the chilly air. There were worse places to be at this moment than Latagnier, Louisiana.

Sunday morning services at Greater Latagnier Fellowship Church of Grace ended right on time during football season. According to the buzz over prechurch coffee in the fellowship hall, the Reverend Simpson achieved two things every Sunday: delivering a message that taught and touched, and ending the service in time to get home for Sunday dinner and football.

Ezra intended to do just that—head back to Calvin's for a foot-long hoagie and four quarters of New Orleans Saints football—just as soon as he completed his mission in the back parking lot.

The thought of his legal file decorating the bottom of Calvin's trash can grated on him. Why couldn't his buddy concentrate on legal maneuvers and let him take care of surveillance and intelligence? After all, those were his specialties.

General Scanlon said he was the best in the department. If he didn't keep his skills sharp, he'd be lost once he returned to work.

That is, if the general still found him useful when this situation was resolved.

The only thing to do was resolve it quickly before he got accustomed to the desk job he was to begin next week. For a man who lived in huts and drank coffee that could double as insecticide, shuffling papers in the Fourth Marine Division's temporary headquarters was an assignment he dreaded.

Another reason to hurry up this process and rid the home of its current inhabitants.

Until last night, Ezra was sure the way to get that accomplished was to pursue legal channels. Then God got hold of him as he lay on Calvin's sleeper sofa in the converted den, and now he wasn't sure of anything. If only his prayers could have been answered, there wouldn't be a need for any further conversations with Sophie Comeaux.

Checking his watch, he frowned. What was taking them so long?

He looked toward the back entrance, a dark-paneled door set into a wall of glass and nearly hidden by the giant magnolias on either side of the walkway. The day he planted those trees with his grandfather rolled across his mind, and he smiled.

The air hung heavy with the threat of cold winter rain, and Ezra, a boy of no more than twelve or thirteen, was less than thrilled at the prospect of planting trees in the chilly semidarkness. He'd tried every way he could to get out of the job, only to find Pastor Landry determined to ignore his protests.

Twelve magnolias had been planted that day, a direct reference, his grandfather claimed, to the twelve disciples and the twelve tribes of Israel. It took them most of the morning, but they'd placed two at every entrance to the church. The rain held off until the last shovelful of dirt had been set into place. Then, as Ezra raced behind his grandfather for the safety of the big sedan, the bottom fell out, drenching them both.

Granny Nell said they looked like drowned rats, and she fussed over them. Ezra vaguely remembered chicken soup in a mug and hot tea with honey and lemon, along with a blanket around his shoulders and a warm stove. One thing he would never forget, though. Above all other memories, the moment stood out as the first time Ezra had felt like something other than an orphan.

He shook off the recollection with a roll of his shoulders. No sense living in the past. His grandparents were with Jesus now; he'd never know that feeling of coming home to a warm blanket and hot tea again.

The sound of chattering was followed in quick progression by the door opening and the girls spilling out into the fall sunshine. They wore matching dresses today, both red with little black dogs on the skirts. Only their Bibles were different, one pink and the other a bright purple, although both had what looked like a drawing tucked in between the pages.

"Girls, slow down. Ladies do not—"

Sophie must have seen him, for she stopped speaking and walking at the same time. She looked almost frozen in time, a vision in red who matched her daughters. While Amanda and Chloe wore little-girl dresses, Sophie was very much the grown-up in her red suit with her hair down in soft, dark curls around her shoulders.

Seeing her from a distance in a shapeless choir robe during services gave him no hint of what to expect. Thus, the greeting he'd planned froze in his throat, a victim of surprise and. . .reluctant admiration.

The girls skipped toward him, calling his name, while Sophie remained rooted in place beside the magnolias. *Rooted.* The irony of the pun made him chuckle.

"Hello, girls."

Each took his hand, and they began talking at once and probably would have continued indefinitely had their mother not intervened by calling their names. At least the chaos got her moving, for she arrived in time to offer a weak smile and an even weaker greeting before ushering the twins toward a silver van parked a few spaces over.

"Say good-bye to Mr. Landry, girls." She glanced over her shoulder as she clicked off the alarm and caused the door to slide open. "I'm sorry, but we have to go."

Odd, but it seemed as though she couldn't part from his company quickly enough.

Refusing to give voice to his irritation, he took a deep breath and let it out slowly. "What's the hurry?" He watched her help the girls inside the vehicle. "The game doesn't start for another half hour."

Sophie paused to turn and face him. "Game?"

"Football game." He waited for a look of understanding. Nothing. "It was a joke."

"Oh." Sophie seemed to consider further conversation, then obviously thought better of it. "Well, good-bye." With that, she disappeared around the back of the van.

Ezra trotted after her, rounding the back bumper of the van as she reached the driver's-side door. He paused, staying well behind the windows where the girls were watching. Unless she climbed in and threw the van into reverse, he was in no danger here. Any closer to her or the twins and he could no longer claim safety.

Calvin was right, plain and simple. He had to keep his distance until the judge ruled.

"Hold on. Can I talk to you a minute?" Her stare told him to hurry. "It's about next weekend. Saturday, actually."

She reached for the door handle and climbed inside, then closed the door. A moment later she rolled down the window and leaned out to look in his direction. "What about Saturday?"

Ezra took a few steps toward her and stuffed his fists into his pockets. A chill wind danced across the bare skin on the back of his neck, and he suppressed a shiver.

Out of the corner of his eye, he saw the twins watching him. At least the window was tinted and could not be rolled down. He expected the door to fly open any minute, however, so he inched closer to Sophie, determined to state his business and make a hasty departure.

"Saturday is. . .well, it might be a problem."

There, he'd said it. At least he'd said part of it. Surely the woman understood he was trying to bow out gracefully.

One look at her told him she did not.

She climbed out and pointed to the sidewalk, then headed in that direction. Ezra followed at a safe distance. Stopping just short of the curb, Sophie turned around and waited for him to catch up. She seemed to think he had something to say, for she only stood there.

"Yeah, so Saturday," he began, unsure of where the sentence would lead. "I, um, well, my lawyer says. . ."

The wind kicked up and tossed a strand of hair across her face. She tucked it behind her ear and gave him a sideways glance. "The major doesn't want you to be there? Fraternizing with the enemy or something like that?"

He nodded. "Yeah, something like that. How did you know?"

"Simple," she said with a shrug. "Mine thinks the same thing. Told me I couldn't sign anything, not even a paper napkin."

"I see." Was that a hint of amusement in her eyes? Interesting. "Yeah, mine said the same thing. Well, nothing about a paper napkin, but I don't think he has a clue about napkins."

They shared a chuckle, which felt strange and yet nice. Ezra tried to keep his mind on the battle, keep his wits sharp and at the ready, but all he could think of was how lovely Sophie Comeaux looked in red.

And how under other circumstances, he might have found more than a passing interest in spending time with her.

"Mommy, I'm getting cold," Chloe called.

"Me, too," Amanda echoed.

"Coming, girls. Why don't you shut the doors and warm up a bit?" She gave Ezra a pleading look and took a step toward the van. "Sorry, I really need to go."

"Yeah, okay." He stuffed his fists in his pockets and caught a deep breath of cold air, then let it out slowly. "Look—it's not you, okay?"

Sophie froze and turned around slowly. "What are you talking about?"

"The house. The lawsuit. You know, the. . ."

Dark eyes glared at him. "The FOR SALE sign? The eviction notice? The summons for court?"

"Yeah," was all he could say as he looked away. Odd, but shame burned in his gut.

He heard her take a step toward him on the crunchy gravel and looked her way. She held her arms across her chest as if protecting her heart.

"Well, if it's not me, then who or what is it, Ezra?"

Cringing, he searched for an answer.

"Oh, there you are, dears."

Ezra looked past Sophie to see Miss Emmeline Trahan heading their way. *Great. Get out now, or you'll miss the first quarter.*

"Afternoon, Miss Trahan," he said. "I was just leaving."

Miss Trahan picked up her pace. "Oh no, you can't leave yet. We now have a quorum, and there are decisions to be made."

nineteen

"Decisions?" Sophie shook her head. "Miss Emmeline, what are you talking about?"

The church secretary fanned her ample bosom with a lace-trimmed hankie that looked remarkably like the ones Granny Nell carried. She gave Ezra a smile, then turned to Sophie.

"The founders' festival, of course. Now I see you've got the twins in the car, so what do you say about coming back inside where it's warm and reconvening this meeting in the fellowship hall? Last night's Warner-Wiggins wedding party left a fridge full of goodies. I'm sure we could make a delicious meal from what's there."

"Oh, I don't know," Ezra said. "I kind of need to get back on the road."

"I understand completely, young man," she said. "I'm a Saints fan myself. Would it help if I told you there's a television set in the pastor's study? I'll have you home by halftime."

"Hold on. I'm still confused." Sophie shook her head. "Miss Emmeline, what are you talking about?"

"Why, Nell's program, of course. You said you needed help."

"Yes," Sophie said, "but what does *he* have to do with it?"

"He's your help, dear." She chuckled. "Isn't that just a hoot? Who knew I could convince Nell's only living relative to participate? I am very grateful, Major Landry."

"Just Ezra," he said, "and you didn't tell me *she* would be part of this."

"Oh my, didn't I?" Miss Emmeline shook her head. "Well now, how could I have let that tidbit slip?"

His tone told her Ezra was just as unhappy about the arrangement as she. Funny, Miss Emmeline didn't seem to understand at all. At least her expression never gave it away if she did. Surely she'd heard about the trouble between them.

Emmeline linked arms with Sophie, then reached for Ezra's hand. "Come—let's focus on what's important here. Family."

"All right," Ezra said. "I'm willing to honor my grandmother any way I can. Why don't the two of you make all the decisions, then just let me know what to do?"

"Mommy," Chloe called, "I'm freezing."

"Yeah," Amanda added, "we're turning into popsicles."

"Coming, girls." Sophie shrugged. "I really need to leave now, but how about you two make the decisions and let me know what my part is?" She turned her attention to Ezra. "After all, the major here is *family*."

"Yes, but you were family to Nell, as well," Miss Emmeline said. "I recall on many occasions how Nell would go on and on about how blessed she was to have you and the girls right next door in case she needed something. Said it made her feel like she had a family again."

Ezra's face paled, but he said nothing.

"And those girls, Ezra—I must tell you I hadn't seen Nell so excited about young people under her roof since you came to live with her and the reverend. Oh, how I remember that day." She touched Sophie's sleeve. "You should have seen him. He's clean-cut now, but back then he had hair down to here."

She pointed to her shoulders. Sophie laughed at the thought of Ezra Landry with anything other than a regulation marine cut.

"She's exaggerating," Ezra said.

"I'm being generous, Ezra Landry, and I've got the pictures to prove it. Would you like me to go home and find them?"

"No, ma'am," he said softly. "You can just leave them there."

"Anyway," Miss Emmeline continued, "he might have been a bit of a rebel, but he was the spitting image of his daddy, Nell's baby brother, and she felt like he was an answer to prayer when the reverend found him in the state orphans home."

"I didn't know that," Ezra said.

Sophie swung her gaze to the marine, who looked as if he'd been blindsided.

"Yes, dear. Of course. But then I don't suppose you could have known that our whole Sunday school class had been praying for you since before you were born. After your daddy took sick and your mama died, why, we were just about out of our minds with worry."

This news seemed to glance off him like an arrow off armor. He took a half step back, releasing himself from Miss Emmeline's grip. Was she mistaken, or did she see a shimmer of tears in his eyes?

"Ezra comes from bayou people, Sophie. Nell's family goes way back in the history of Latagnier. Her daddy was a preacher here, and so was her granddaddy before him. Married half the parish, the Reverend Broussard did, and probably buried just as many before his untimely passing. Lost him to the flu, we did, and his wife, too. Poor soul had just delivered Ezra's daddy. He was a late-in-life baby, you know. For years we thought Nell was to be an only child."

"That's so sad. What happened to Nell and the baby?"

"Oh, Nell must have been fifteen at the time, maybe a bit older. Practically of marrying age, I remember that. We all wanted to take them in, but Nell's grandmother on her mama's side insisted on moving them to Dallas, after she sold everything they owned and put it in her own bank account. Next thing we knew, both of 'em were at the Buckner Home and their grandmother was living in Highland Park in a brand-new home."

"No wonder Nell had such a heart for orphans."

"Oh, indeed." Miss Emmeline smiled. "Soon as she was old enough, Nell took little Robbie and moved back here. Went to work cleaning the church and ended up marrying the pastor. She used to joke that the only reason the reverend proposed was to save the cleaning fees and make the church budget balance."

This time Ezra chuckled. "That sounds like Granny Nell."

"He was a good man, Rev. Landry, and a fine preacher. Quite a bit older than Nell, he was, but he adored that woman. He did many good things for the church, too. Planted those magnolias for one. You helped him with that, didn't you?"

"Yes, ma'am," he said softly.

"And Ezra's daddy, he was a good man, too. He just came back from the war with a nervous condition, that's all."

"Yeah, lack of booze made him nervous."

"Ezra Landry, I won't have you disrespecting your elders." She softened her features. "Now, since our girls seem to be a bit anxious. . ."

Sophie turned her attention to the van where the windows had fogged up. Hearts and flowers decorated the opaque surface, along with a message scribbled backward in large letters: HELP! WE ARE FREZIN TO DEATH.

Embarrassment heated Sophie's cheeks. "I'm terribly sorry. I really need to speak to the girls. Could we talk on the phone, perhaps, Miss Emmeline? You can let me know what you and Ezra decide."

"Well, I suppose." She clapped her hands and smiled. "What am I thinking? We can table this discussion until this weekend's barbecue."

Sophie blinked hard and pasted on a broad smile to cover her surprise. "This weekend?"

Miss Emmeline nodded. "Of course. The whole church will be there. We wouldn't miss it for the world. Tell the girls their invitation was delightful."

"Their invitation?" She cast a quick glance at the van. "They gave you an invitation to the barbecue Saturday?"

"Yes, dear, weren't they supposed to?"

"Well, um." She paused to refocus and readjust her smile. "Of course. I'm happy there will be a nice turnout."

With that, she made good her escape, slipping into the van before she let her smile fall. "Girls," she said as she closed the door and swiveled to face them, "what's this I hear about the entire church being invited to our house this Saturday?"

"I told Chloe we should ask first," Amanda said.

"Chloe?" Sophie turned her attention to the elder twin. "Something you want to say?"

"Mommy, you said that I could invite anyone I wanted, remember?"

"I did?"

Both girls nodded in unison.

"All right, so how did the entire church get invited?"

"That was Amanda," Chloe said.

"Amanda?"

The little girl grinned. "I used the printer all by myself this morning while you were getting ready for church."

"You did? That's wonderful." Sophie paused. "But what does that have to do with inviting the entire church to our barbecue?"

"I just wanted to make one copy to give to my friend Courtney. But I guess I pushed number one too many times."

"She pushed 111, not 1," Chloe said. "So we took them to Sunday school and gave them to our teacher."

Sophie leaned back in her seat and groaned. "You brought 111 invitations to church?"

"No, Mommy," Amanda said. "I saved one for Courtney. She was sick today."

Sophie turned the key and cranked the engine, then adjusted the temperature up a notch. "Chloe, please use the towel behind your seat to clean off the writing on the window. I don't think you need rescuing from the cold anymore."

Tap. Tap. Tap.

Sophie jumped, then turned toward the sound to find Ezra standing beside the van. A push of the lever and the window lowered, letting in the chilly air.

Great. "Yes?"

Ezra stood ramrod straight, his face expressionless. "About that barbecue. What should I bring?"

twenty

"What are you doing?"

Ezra looked up from his work to offer Calvin a smile. "Making apple pie."

Calvin set his briefcase on the table, then shrugged out of his jacket and placed it across the back of the chair. He approached with a caution more appropriate to watching a bomb being diffused than a pie being constructed.

"I couldn't find your cutting board, so I made one out of stuff I found in the garage. I hope that was okay."

"Yeah." Calvin shook his head. "You're chopping apples."

"Sure am." Ezra reached for another apple from the bag. "Something wrong, Cal?"

"Only that I have no idea what's come over you." He walked around the bar to climb atop the nearest stool. Resting his elbows on the counter, he cradled his chin in his hands. "Since when do you bake pies?"

"I don't know. I guess since today." He sliced the apple in half and laid each piece on the board. "I think of it as similar to cleaning deer or fish. See?"

With practiced motions he used the knife to cut the apple halves, then began the process of peeling them. The core and peel went into the trash, and the apple slices fell into the bowl beside him.

"Nothing to it. Want to try, Cal?"

Calvin shook his head. "No, thanks. Besides, you're doing it wrong."

"Doing what wrong?"

"Peeling that apple wrong. You take the skin off first, then chop it."

For the next few minutes, Ezra argued the finer points of

112

apple peeling with Calvin. Finally Calvin rolled up his sleeves and jumped off the stool to join Ezra at the counter.

"Hand me that knife." He pointed to a wood-handled knife in the center of the knife block. "Now stand aside."

"Hold it." Ezra planted his feet and dared the lawyer to enter his domain. "I'm not giving up my position to a guy who makes a living behind a desk. Stand aside yourself, pal."

"Excuse me, Major Landry. Where are you reporting for duty next week? I have it on good authority they are getting a *desk* ready for you on my floor."

"That's temporary, Cal, okay? General Scanlon said he's got something for me at the Pentagon if I choose not to go back into the field. It just has to go through channels. You know how long that takes."

"Yeah, longer than it will take for me to show you how to bake a pie—that's how long."

"Oh, you are just begging for me to show you up, aren't you?"

"Am I?"

"Yeah, and I can and will. Only let's make this a little sweeter. Whoever makes the best pie wins."

"Wins what?"

Ezra shrugged. "Who cares?"

"You got a deal. Wait. Who's going to decide?"

"What about Sophie Comeaux and that lady lawyer of hers?"

"That's not fair," Calvin said. "What qualifies them to judge an apple pie?"

"Think about it, Cal. They hate us both; thus we are on equal footing. I can't think of anything more fair."

"So I have to change my mind about allowing you to go to that woman's barbecue?"

"No, you don't have to change your mind. We're not going as guests. We're going as competitors."

Calvin thought a minute, then grinned. "Deal."

He retrieved a bowl from the cabinet and dumped half the apples into it. Opening the cabinet next to the oven, Calvin pulled out a black apron emblazoned with the marine logo.

"I have nine, and you have nine," Calvin said. "Set aside what you've already done, and let's race. We'll see who's the man around here."

"The man?" Ezra doubled over with laughter. "You're wearing an apron, Cal. One look at the two of us and it's obvious who the *man* is."

"That's right," Calvin said. "The *man* is the one without the stain on his shirt. Now buck up, Marine, and prepare to be bested."

Ezra looked down at the streak of flour and spots of vanilla decorating the front of his denim shirt. Eyes narrowed, he set his bead on the competition.

"It's every man for himself then. Got a spare apron?"

❧

"Major Landry? General Scanlon's on the horn."

"Thank you, Corporal." Ezra set aside the security brief from Quantico and picked up the phone. "Hello, General Scanlon. Major Landry here."

"Landry, you finished with that nonsense that took you off my payroll?"

The chair protested as he leaned back. "Actually, sir, the matter is still in progress."

"You know I don't work like that. Give it to me straight. Are you coming back or not?"

"Sir, I have every intention of coming back as soon as—"

General Scanlon let loose an expletive. "What I hear is that you're gonna be offered a promotion and some fancy desk job at the Pentagon. That true?"

Promotion? To lieutenant colonel? His father's rank. The one Robert Boudreaux claimed Ezra would never achieve.

Ezra took a deep breath and let it out slowly. "Sir," he said with as little excitement as he could manage, "you probably know more about that than I do. Right now I'm just pushing papers and praying my legal troubles end soon."

"Well, if you weren't so good at what you do, I'd have

shipped you out. You know patience isn't my strong suit."

"Yes, sir, and I'm having some trouble with it myself."

"Son, I need to ask you something, and I want you to be straight-up honest with me. Is there a reason you're not shooting for that promotion?"

"No, sir." He glanced at the open door and waved as Calvin walked in.

"Then what's the problem?"

"The problem is that I like what I do, sir. The work suits me."

Calvin eased into the chair across from him. Ezra wrote a note letting him know who was on the other end of the line, causing Calvin to grimace.

"I'm going to give you a piece of advice, not as your commanding officer but as a man who has lived a lot longer than you and learned a few things along the way." He paused. "I know you are the best man in my company. I've seen you lead others more times than I can count, and I know you're good at it. Ever think of ditching all the glamour jobs and teaching?"

"Teaching?" He shook his head. "I don't understand, sir."

"What's not to understand? How many languages do you speak?"

"Seventeen."

"And how many tours abroad have you taken since you finished OCS?"

"Four."

"And tell me this: How many times did you find yourself showing everyone else on the mission how to do their jobs?"

Ezra chuckled. More than once he'd had to report to the general that he'd been sent unqualified men and had to bring their skills up to par. "So you're saying I missed my calling and should have become a drill instructor?"

The general chuckled. "Hardly. You and I both know there are schools turning out men just like you for missions like the ones you've been completing for years. You learned from someone. Now consider going back and teaching fellow marines what you know."

"I'll consider it, sir."

A few minutes later, Ezra hung up the phone. "That was strange."

Calvin stretched his legs out in front of him. "What?"

"General Scanlon wants me to be a teacher."

"Interesting." Calvin shrugged. "Junior high or high school?"

"Very funny. Try special ops training."

"Ooh, secret stuff." He wiggled his fingers. "So classified they don't even know about it."

"Yeah, something like that. So any progress on this house thing?" He gave his friend a sideways look. "I mean, assuming you retrieved the file from the trash and are continuing to work on it."

Calvin ignored the jibe to shake his head. They both knew Calvin's action had been more of an attention-getting gesture than anything else. As much as he protested, Calvin wouldn't walk away from a case.

"Looks as if the judge is in no hurry to set another hearing date. I have a call in to the court, but I don't know what good that will do. If I didn't know better, I would have to wonder if God's trying to tell us something."

"Why's that?"

"I've seen some quirky civilian judges in my time, but I've never seen one procrastinate on a hearing date like this one." He paused. "I don't know. Maybe the timing's just not right."

"Well, pal, time's something I don't have a lot of. The general's getting tired of waiting for me. Then there's the Pentagon job. General Scanlon told me he heard I was the front runner."

"Congratulations, pal. That's a promotion, isn't it?"

"To lieutenant colonel."

twenty-one

October 9

"I'm here. Now let's get this party started." Bree strolled into the kitchen wearing a vibrant orange ensemble and carrying two shopping bags along with her matching orange purse. "You can go change now."

"Hey," Sophie said. "This is what I'm wearing."

"That's what I was afraid of." She deposited her bags on the table, then riffled through the nearest one until she found what she was looking for. "Ta da!" she exclaimed as she pulled out a pair of jeans and what looked like a garment more fit for Amanda or Chloe than an adult. "Come on. Let's see how it looks on you."

Before Sophie could protest, Bree led her down the hall to her bedroom. She thrust the clothes into Sophie's hands, then pointed toward the bathroom.

"Go. Now. You have no time to argue."

"What's wrong with what I'm wearing?"

Bree smiled. "Nothing at all, honey. I wear baggy jeans and sweatshirts, too, but not in public and especially not at parties. Please just give these a try. I promise they're very tasteful."

Doubtful but curious, Sophie closeted herself in the bathroom and slid off her favorite jeans and sweatshirt, then reached for the outfit. A moment later she stood back and stared at the woman in the mirror.

The jeans fit as if they'd been made for her, not loose and broken in like her other pair but not so tight as to be indecent either. And the top, its jewel-tone colors and soft-draped neck flattered yet covered while the tucks at the waist fit nicely.

It was nothing she would ever buy for herself. Still, Sophie

117

had to admit she liked the result.

A quick knock and Bree tumbled in, a pair of black strappy sandals dangling from her hand. "I couldn't wait to see how you—"

She froze. Silence reigned.

"Okay, that's it. I shouldn't have listened to you. Hand me those clothes. I don't have time to play around."

Bree scooped up the offending garments and stuffed them into the hamper. "Oh, I don't think so. Sophie, you look gorgeous. Don't move. Wait—put these on." She thrust the sandals at Sophie, then scampered away only to return seconds later with her handbag. "Go over by the mirror."

Sophie struggled to buckle the left shoe, then stood. "I think the last time I wore heels I was at the prom. No, wait, my college graduation."

"Well, it's high time you fixed that lapse in fashion. Now come over here and let me see what I can do with that hair. It's lovely, by the way, but it just needs a little help. Oh, and those cheeks need some color."

In the span of ten minutes, Bree remedied her lack of proper makeup and twisted her hair into a loose bun, leaving soft tendrils around her face and down her back. A stranger stared back at her from the mirror.

"Mommy?" Chloe stood in the bathroom door, a smile on her face. "Amanda, come see Mommy."

"Ooh, Mommy, you look so pretty," Amanda said. "You don't look old anymore."

"Out of the mouths of babes," Bree said. "Come on, girls— I need your help making bouquets for the centerpieces. Think you're up to that?"

Off they went, down the hall toward the backyard. Bree remained at the door, however.

Sophie turned away from the stranger to smile at her friend. "Something wrong?"

"No," she said. "Not anymore, that is."

"What do you mean?"

Bree shook her head. "Honey, I love you like a sister. You know that, right?"

She nodded. "Yeah, I know that."

"Then will you understand when I tell you that I'm worried about you?"

"Why?"

Bree touched Sophie's curls. "Because I'm afraid you've forgotten how to have fun."

"Auntie Bree!"

"Coming, darlings," she called before turning her attention back to Sophie. "Remember what life was like before you gave up on love?"

"I didn't give up. . . ." She let the words hang there, knowing they weren't true. "All right, maybe I did. But I'm much happier now. No disappointments, no broken hearts."

"And where was God in this decision, Soph? Did you consult Him before you closed off your heart?"

"I'm not you, Bree. I don't seem to roll with the punches the way you do." She offered a wry smile. "I certainly don't have the way with men that you do. Any advice? I mean, I do have over a hundred people coming over for dinner. What if I'm forced to have an actual conversation with an eligible male?"

Bree shook her head. "Be yourself, Sophie. Be who God created you to be."

"That's it?"

"Isn't that enough?"

Ding dong.

"Auntie Bree!"

"You get the door, Sophie, and I'll handle the kids."

Sophie started out on uncertain footing, but by the time she got to the door, she'd recalled the proper way to walk in heels. Like riding a bicycle.

She opened the door to find Ezra and his attorney standing on her porch. Neither looked particularly happy to be there, although the attorney wore a more sour expression than his client.

Both had donned jeans for the occasion, although the lawyer's were pressed and starched while Ezra had obviously opted for comfort. The attorney's button-down look proved a counterpoint for Ezra's maroon Marine Corps sweatshirt and sneakers.

"Come in," she managed over the tightening sensation in her stomach. "What do you have there?"

"Apple pies." Ezra pressed past without further comment to her. "Kitchen's this way, Cal, but you might as well leave yours on the front porch."

Sophie teetered behind them on her heels, making sure not to trip as she rounded the corner. "Just set them on the counter."

The attorney gave the room a cursory glance, then turned his attention to Sophie. "Two things. First, my apologies for being early. My client was a little lead-footed."

"I drove the speed limit," Ezra said. "Not that you noticed for all your complaining."

"Second," he said, "I am here under protest. Ezra seems to think it appropriate to socialize despite ongoing litigation, but I don't."

"And third," Ezra added, "he doesn't have a clue how to bake a decent apple pie."

"Now wait just a minute. It's you who has no clue how to bake an apple pie." He turned to Sophie. "I'll be honest with you, Miss Comeaux."

"The world's first honest lawyer," Ezra interjected before giving his friend a playful shove.

Calvin shoved back but otherwise looked completely undisturbed. "As I was saying, Ezra convinced me to accompany him despite grave reservations on my part. The real reason I'm here is to show him my pie is much better than anything he could dream up in his feeble mind."

Ezra doubled over with laughter. "Is that so? Well, Sophie, just so you know, my pie is an old family recipe. I think you will find it has exceptional flavor and a superior crust."

He said that last part in what she assumed was a dead-on imitation of his friend Calvin.

"Well, why don't we just set our pies out and let Miss Comeaux decide which is best."

"It's Sophie, and no, thank you. I don't believe I will judge these pies. Why don't we let the guests decide?"

"Hey, Soph, you have any more garden shears? These don't seem to be—" Bree stopped in her tracks and broke into a grin. "Well, hello, gentlemen."

"Bree, this is Ezra Landry. He's brought Calvin Dubose with him. Major Dubose, that is.

"Gentlemen, this is Bree Jackson."

"*You're* Bree Jackson?" Calvin's shock was unmistakable. "You sound so different on the phone."

"Different from what, Counselor?" She broadened her smile. "What were you expecting? No, wait. Don't tell me. I'm sure I would be offended."

Ezra's attorney looked flustered. "Yes, well, I suppose. I should apologize."

"Apologies are nice, but a man who can fix garden shears is even better." A moment later Bree had the attorney following her out the back door, shears in hand.

"How did she do that?" Ezra walked to the window and shook his head. "That woman tamed the mighty beast in under sixty seconds. You wouldn't believe how much he complained on the drive over here." He turned to face her. "That's why we got here so quickly."

Sophie shrugged. "Happens all the time. I think it's one of her spiritual gifts."

"Interesting." He gave her a strange look. "Something's different. Your hair."

She patted her messy do and contemplated running from the room to repair the damage. To that end she took a step backward.

"It looks. . .um, nice." The statement seemed to cost him as he leaned back against the counter. Clapping his hands, he straightened. "So what can I do to help you with the barbecue?"

Nice? Did he say she looked nice?

Sophie smoothed the front of her sweater and shifted positions. Their gazes locked, and for a moment she let go of the idea that this man was her enemy in favor of seeing him as a man.

"It's not necessary, really."

He walked toward her, and her heart did a flip-flop. When he brushed past her to reach for the salad ingredients Bree had left on the table, Sophie inhaled deeply of his aftershave, then felt guilty. *He is the man trying to evict you, idiot.*

"How about I make the salad?" he asked.

"Sure. I never did learn how to do that very well."

"Knives?"

She walked over to the cutlery drawer and opened it. "Which one?"

Ezra leaned in close. "The sharpest one."

Again she inhaled. This time no guilt followed. The man certainly smelled nice.

"No sharp knives in this kitchen. I've got little ones." She looked up into dark eyes that were far too close for comfort. "Sorry."

The eyes blinked. "I think I can make do."

"Suit yourself." She stepped back and reached for the boiled eggs, praying over the next words she would speak. "I'm glad you decided to come. I hope you don't feel uncomfortable here."

He set the knife down and turned to face her. "You mean that, don't you?"

twenty-two

"I do mean it, Ezra." Sophie placed the eggs on the counter and reached into the cabinet beneath it for the stockpot. She set the pot in the sink, positioning it under the faucet.

Chloe rounded the corner and launched herself into the marine's arms. Amanda followed suit, leaving Ezra with a seven-year-old on each arm.

"Hey there, girls," he said as he twirled them around before setting them back on their feet. "Wow! That was quite a greeting."

"We finished your present," Chloe said. "Want me to get it?"

"Me, too?" Amanda said.

"Sure." He watched them race down the hall only to return seconds later and hand him a package wrapped in brown paper that had once been a grocery bag. It was now covered in ribbons, glitter, and drawings made by both girls.

"Open it," Amanda said as she skittered to Sophie's side.

"All right, I will."

He pulled out a chair and settled at the dining table, placing the gift in front of him. Chloe seated herself beside him. Being careful not to tear the wrapping, he slowly revealed a brown book.

"It's Granny Nell's diary," Amanda said.

"Her journal," Chloe corrected. "One of them anyway. She had lots on account of she's old, but this is the one she wanted you to have."

"How do you know that?"

"She told us that day on the porch," Amanda said. "That day she went to her house for cookies and didn't come back until Mommy found her reading her Bible to Jesus."

"She wasn't reading her Bible to Jesus, Amanda. You always

get that wrong. She was reading her Bible when Jesus came and took her with Him." Chloe's expression softened. "We didn't go to the funeral 'cause we're gonna see her someday in heaven."

"Mommy said we needed to remember her alive because the lady in the box wasn't our Granny Nell. That was just her earth suit." Amanda looked up at Sophie for confirmation. "Her best parts are in heaven."

"That's right, baby." She squeezed her daughter's hand. "They sure are."

Ezra leafed through the book, then turned his attention to Sophie. "Did you know about this?"

"We kept it a secret, even from Mommy, because it was supposed to be a surprise," Chloe said. "Mommy only lets us keep secrets about presents. Those are good secrets so it's okay."

"Sounds like your mommy is right." He closed the cover and placed the folded wrapping paper inside. "This is very special, girls. Thank you very much."

Amanda crossed the kitchen to stand beside Ezra. "It was Granny Nell's idea. She made us promise. And my mommy says you never make a promise unless you're going to do it."

"Girls," Bree called, "are you coming back out here? I need some more help."

The twins raced back outside, leaving Sophie with mixed emotions. All at once she wanted to smile and cry. Ezra seemed to be dealing with the same issue as he blinked hard and swiped at his eyes with the backs of his hands.

"I told you when I invited you that I believed if you got to know the girls and me you would see what your grandmother meant to us. And what we meant to her. I didn't know what the girls had planned, though, and that's the truth."

Ezra's expression went from confused to something Sophie couldn't quite define. "So you aren't going to try to talk me out of the lawsuit?"

"Honestly?" Sophie hit the hot-water faucet and watched as the stockpot began to fill. "I don't think I will have to."

"Oh?" He grinned and pointed outside where Bree had the stoic attorney laughing and arranging flowers in a vase. "You're not going to sic her on me, are you? Wait. You already did."

"Only in self-defense, Ezra. You started it. I'm just trying to show you there's another option."

He seemed to consider her statement. "That's where we differ, Sophie."

They stood there like a couple of idiots until the bell rang. "Doorbell," Sophie said.

"Yes," Ezra said. "Doorbell."

"Would you excuse me?" Sophie grabbed the dish towel and wiped her hands.

"Wait."

Ezra caught her arm as she walked past, and her unsteady heels gave way. She stumbled and fell into his arms. In a swift motion, he righted her and took a step backward. The look on his face was pure shock.

"I'm really sorry, Sophie. I didn't mean to—"

"Well, isn't this nice? I see you two are getting acquainted." Sophie looked past Ezra to find Miss Emmeline standing in the doorway with a Bundt cake. "I hope you don't mind. The doorbell must be broken. I let myself in."

"Oh, no, of course," Sophie said.

Ding-dong.

Miss Emmeline grinned. "Guess the doorbell fixed itself. Why don't I go answer it while you two go back to whatever you were doing?"

"Actually I was making a salad," Ezra said a bit too quickly.

"And I was boiling eggs."

The church secretary gave them an amused look. "Of course you were, my dears," she said as she headed toward the door, giggling. "Young people these days," she said as she opened the door and shouted a greeting.

"That went well," Sophie muttered as she followed Miss Emmeline to the door, kicking her dangerous heels under the sofa as she passed by.

Soon guests filled the house and spilled into the backyard. Sophie shuffled plates of food to make room on the counter, then gave up and moved the buffet to the picnic table. Thankfully the weather was mild, just as the weatherman predicted. By the time the stars began to dot the sky and the floodlight came on, folks had settled into groups and were enjoying the evening.

Mr. Arceneaux from the Dip Cone brought his fiddle, and the boys from Latagnier Auto were warming up to play on the makeshift stage in the corner of the yard. In all, the evening had been exhausting but wonderful.

Sophie joined Bree and the girls at the back step and half listened as her friend entertained her daughters with stories of her childhood. "And they even made us work in the garden."

"Ugh. Mommy says she will do that, too, if we ever have a garden that grows something besides weeds." Sophie looked up to see that Ezra had joined their group.

"What's wrong with a garden that grows weeds?" Ezra tickled Amanda, then Chloe. "I happen to think weeds are some of the more low-maintenance plants in today's gardening world."

When the girls giggled, he continued. "Say, did you have any of that salad I made?"

"Yes. Was it made from weeds?" Chloe asked before succumbing to a fit of giggles.

"Well, as a matter of fact, it was."

Both girls squealed.

"I wondered why it tasted so good," Bree said. "You must have removed all the bitterroot. That one always ruins things. Bitterness generally does, you know."

He looked for a moment as though he might comment in depth. Then Ezra shook his head. "Pun intended?"

"I'll let you decide." Bree grasped the twins' hands. "Come— let's see what we can find on the dessert table. I think Mrs. Gentry brought homemade ice cream. It's not pistachio, but I hear it's pretty good."

Sophie watched Bree lead the girls to the picnic table, then cast a glance back in her direction. She was surprised to see Ezra settle in their place.

"I've been talking to Miss Emmeline, or rather she's been talking to me."

She leaned forward to see his face. "About?"

"This Founders' Day thing. She has some ideas she wants to run past us, but first we need to discuss our plans."

"Ah." Sophie studied her short nails. "But we have no plans."

"That's the point. I think we should get some plans. Maybe meet and talk about it."

"Sure."

The music rose, silencing their conversation. Sophie leaned back against the rail and let the melody transport her to a time when her daddy let her dance in his arms to this very song. Eyes closed, she moved her bare feet in time with the waltz.

When the music stopped, she opened them again and found Ezra staring at her. "Where were you just now?"

"What?" She shook her head and straightened her posture. "I don't know. Why?"

"Because I think that's the first time I've ever seen you at peace."

Sophie pushed a tendril of hair from her eyes. "I'm not usually this stressed out." She fixed her gaze on Ezra. "I've had some rather worrisome things going on. Lawsuits, evictions, and such."

To his credit Ezra ducked his head. "Yeah, I guess you have."

Several couples from the church approached in a group. "Lovely evening, Sophie. Thank you for inviting us," one of the men said.

"We'll say our good nights early," another added. "The alarm clock will be going off way too soon."

Ezra checked his watch after they left. "It's only seven thirty. Even Calvin over there can make it until nine.

"Hey, Cal, dish me up some of that homemade vanilla, would you? No frills or toppings, just the ice cream." He nudged Sophie. "Want some?"

"No, thanks. I'm stuffed."

"Suit yourself. Just one," he called to Calvin. "The lady's stuffed."

"Oh, great. Did you have to say that out loud?"

Sophie looked past Ezra to the picnic table. Calvin had joined Bree and the girls and was currently decorating their ice cream with sprays of whipped cream from a can he held high. To the delight of the girls, he occasionally squirted a bit of the cream into their open palms.

"Looks like the lawyers have set their briefcases aside for the night." Ezra glanced up at the moon, then back at Sophie. "Maybe we ought to set aside our differences, too. Temporarily," he added hastily.

"Temporarily? Like a truce?"

He shook his head. "Actually I was thinking more like a cease-fire."

"Until when?"

Ezra sighed. "That's the funny thing about cease-fires. They can last indefinitely."

twenty-three

"Soph, can you handle things? I'm going to catch a ride with Calvin since my car's making that funny noise again." She paused to smile at Calvin. "Normally I would walk, but since it's dark, Calvin would rather see me home safely."

Bree stood in the kitchen with a grin and a pleading look. Behind her was the formerly somber and smartly dressed Major Dubose. He now wore a broad smile and a mustard stain just below his collar.

"Sure, go on. I'm fine. I've got it all under control. That's the beauty of paper plates."

Ezra strolled through carrying four black garbage bags. "I'm heading for the curb. Any more trash in here?"

Sophie handed him the bag full of soiled plates, napkins, and cups. "That's the last of it. I'm done. The kitchen is officially closed. I'll walk you out."

She trailed the pair to the porch, then leaned against the railing while Calvin opened the car door for Bree and helped her in. While Calvin trotted around to climb into the driver's seat, Ezra walked back to the porch. He reached to shake her hand, then held it instead.

"Tell the girls again how much I appreciate their gift, would you?"

She forced her attention away from the feel of her hand in his. "You already did a good job of letting them know, Ezra."

He nodded. For a moment she thought Ezra might say more. Rather, he smiled. Still, he held tight to her hand.

"Thank you for inviting me."

"And thank you for coming. I hope you've seen what you needed to see."

"I'll admit it wasn't what I expected." Almost imperceptibly his grip tightened. "Not at all."

Under the porch light, his hair looked lighter, his eyes darker. His square chin still held a defiant pose, but the smile on his lips was nearly gone.

"Did we disappoint you?"

"Unfortunately, yes."

She plucked her hand from his grasp and wrapped her arms around her chest, taking a step back as she absorbed the news. "I'm terribly sorry, Ezra. I hoped we might have helped you to understand what life is like here in this house. What we are like."

He stepped toward her, hands at his side. "That's just the problem, Sophie," he said. "You have."

"Hey, Marine," Calvin called, "time to retreat."

Ezra looked over his shoulder to nod. "Be right there." When he returned his attention to Sophie, he wore a confused look. "I don't know how you did it, but you talked me into being here tonight without saying a word. And I have to tell you: I risked losing my lawyer over this."

Tracing the groove on the porch railing with her forefinger, she avoided his scrutinizing gaze. "Really? How did I do that?"

Straightening his shoulders, he leaned in her direction. "Back at church when you, well, never mind. You just did."

Sophie felt the oddest urge to give the man a hug. "Oh," she gasped as good sense overtook her. "You're forgetting the journal. I'll go get it."

By the time she retrieved the journal and the two clean pie pans off the table, the urge had mostly passed and logic prevailed. Ezra Landry was her opponent in this battle to keep a roof over her girls' heads. Sure, under other conditions, she might have given him a second glance, but even then the fact that he was a marine would have stopped her cold.

No, she'd get over this odd attraction to him by morning. The feelings surging in her were obviously a trick of the night and a result of her long and exhausting day.

She stepped onto the porch to find him waiting in the same spot where she left him. Wiping her free hand on the back of her jeans, she crossed the old wooden boards.

"I found these, too," she said as she handed him the pie pans along with the journal.

Ezra chuckled. "Calvin and I forgot all about the competition. Guess we'll never know whose pie was best."

"Guess not," she said.

He took a step forward and looked down into her eyes. "You liked mine best, didn't you?"

While the gesture was clearly meant to be funny, Sophie felt no humor. Rather, her mouth went dry and her mind blank. He stood close, this man she should despise, and then closer.

"Um, Sophie," he whispered, now so close she could smell the peppermint on his breath.

"Um, what?" was the only response she could manage.

"Tell me you liked mine best. I know you did." He inched closer. "I was watching you when you went back for seconds."

She lifted slightly onto her tiptoes. "Watching me? Really?"

"Good night, Sophie." Without looking back, Ezra bounded down the stairs to the driveway to wedge himself sideways into the car's nearly nonexistent rear seat. "Was that necessary?" Sophie heard him shout.

Calvin responded with a resounding "Yes."

Any further conversation was swallowed up in the roar of the car engine as it headed down the street. She'd have to get the full report from Bree in the morning.

When the muscle car disappeared around the corner, Sophie wandered back inside and locked the door. It had been a lovely night, one she'd never have planned for in a million years.

She checked the back door, then headed down the hall to bed, stopping at the open door to the girls' room. They had been so tired that she put them to bed in their party clothes. Now Amanda lay on her side, her stuffed pig cuddled in the crook of her arm, while Chloe lay on her stomach, her face half buried in her pillow.

"Thank You, Lord," she whispered, "for this dwelling place and the precious souls beneath its roof and for the dear one who now lives with You. Thank You for best friends who make me look like Cinderella for an evening and for little girls who accidentally invite the whole church to dinner."

Settling under the covers that night, she remembered one last reason to give thanks. "And, Lord, thank You for cease-fires. Is it too much to ask of You that this one lasts indefinitely?"

twenty-four

October 10

Ezra arrived at 421 Riverside Avenue at a quarter to two with the two items essential for the job: a good shovel and his heavy-duty gloves. It might be a Sunday afternoon during football season, but he had a mission that was much more important than watching a game on television. The garden in the backyard of 421A was in dire need.

He'd planned to offer Sophie and the girls lunch after church, until he saw Sophie walking to her van with the owner of the Dip Cone. Rather than embarrass himself in front of the Arceneaux fellow, Ezra hit a drive-through, then headed for Calvin's place to change clothes and pick up supplies.

Now he sat in the car in front of the house, trying to figure out whether to ring the doorbell or just walk around to the back and start to work at it. Amanda took the decision away from him when she burst out of the front door calling his name.

"Hey, squirt," he called.

"Did you come to see my mommy?"

Ezra popped the trunk and climbed out of the car. "What makes you think that?"

"Ezra?" Sophie stood on the porch, shielding her eyes from the afternoon sun. "Is that you?"

"Yes, it's me." He retrieved the shovel and his gloves and slammed the trunk, then crossed the yard toward her.

"What are you doing here?"

"Just thought I'd get some work done in the yard," he said when he reached the porch. "Is that a problem?"

She looked skeptical. "Guess not," she said. "Dare I ask why?"

"No, Sophie, you dare not."

Opening the gate, Ezra headed for the backyard and the pitiful excuse for a garden he'd spied at the party last night. A little elbow grease and a regular program of watering along with some amendments to the soil and that garden would bloom in the spring just as Granny Nell's used to.

Funny how he'd signed on willingly for garden duty today, and yet he'd detested the job as a kid. *Well, you're not a kid anymore, Marine.*

Ezra set to work with Chloe and Amanda alternating between watching and jumping on the trampoline. Before long, the girls had volunteered to stuff trash bags with the weeds Ezra pulled. The trio worked well together, and soon the garden began to look like an actual garden.

"Lemonade anyone?" Sophie rounded the corner with a tray of lemonade and a big grin.

Tossing Ezra a towel, she set the tray on the picnic table, then poured four glasses. Amanda and Chloe took theirs right away, downed the drinks, and let out loud burps.

"Girls, that was disgusting. Where are your manners?"

Ezra seemed to be trying not to laugh, a fact that endeared him to her. The last thing the girls needed was encouragement in those kinds of things.

He walked over, towel slung around his neck, and Sophie couldn't help but smile. He might be the guy trying to evict her, but right now he was the guy with leaves in his hair.

She handed him a glass of lemonade, then pointed to his hair. "Leaves. Let me help you."

Standing on tiptoe, she brushed her hand over the spiky strands until the leaves had fallen. All but one landed on the ground around Ezra. The single reluctant leaf remained stuck to his forehead.

Amanda saw it first and began to giggle, and Chloe followed suit. Ezra pretended to try to remove the leaf only to discover it seemed to be permanently attached. Sophie laughed along with the girls at the marine's antics. When he jumped on the trampoline and called for the girls to join him, Sophie settled onto the porch step to watch.

"Oh no, you don't," he called to her. "Come join us hard-working gardeners."

"Yeah, Mommy," Chloe said. "Come join us."

"Oh, I don't know. That was the girls' birthday present. I've never tried to jump on it."

Ezra stopped and turned to face her, his hands on his hips. "Are you serious? You have a trampoline in your yard, and you don't use it? That's a travesty."

Amanda tugged on Ezra's shirttail. "What's a travesty?"

He sat cross-legged on the trampoline and got eye-to-eye with Amanda. "Honey, that's when a mommy has forgotten how to have fun."

"Hey, I know how to have fun." She rose and put her hands on her hips. "In fact, I'm a pretty fun mom, aren't I, girls?"

Amanda looked at Chloe, then at Ezra. All three of them turned to grin at her. From this angle, the trio looked as if they were related, such were the expressions on their faces.

"Traitors," she said as she kicked off her shoes and headed for the trampoline. "Move out of the way, and you'll see how much fun I am."

Ezra jumped off, then reached for Amanda, swinging her around before setting her on the ground. He did the same with Chloe.

"It's all yours, Sophie." Ezra reached to wrap his hands around her waist and lift her onto the trampoline. "Want me to stand close in case you fall?"

"I'm not going to fall," she said with a bit more bravado than she felt. "Besides, that's what the nets are for."

It was higher than she expected up there, and nothing seemed stable or secure. Sophie gave thanks that she'd gone to the extra expense of placing those guards around the edges, for she might be the one needing them.

The first bounce was a bit higher than she'd anticipated, and the second one left her head spinning. The third, however, landed her on her rear, which set the girls laughing.

"Hey, I meant to do that."

"Sure you did, Mommy," Chloe said with a giggle.

Sophie wobbled to her feet and grinned. "All right, I think I've got it now."

This time she managed four jumps in a row before she stopped of her own volition. "See," she said, "I can do this. Who wants to join me?"

"I do," both girls said at once.

They scrambled toward the trampoline only to find Ezra in their path. "No way, kids. You get to do this all the time. It's my turn."

He climbed onto the trampoline and gave Sophie a wicked grin. "How high do you want to go?"

"What do you mean?"

Ezra looked her up and down, then touched his temple with his forefinger. "You weigh what, a hundred, maybe a hundred and ten?"

One-twenty, but you'll never know that. "None of your business, Ezra."

"All right, well, I'm 175. I'm not up on all the laws of physics, but I'll bet you I can bounce you at least as high as that tree there."

He pointed to a spot that might as well have been the moon. "Oh no, you—"

Before she could finish her response, Ezra leaped into the air and came down hard on the surface of the trampoline. Sophie shot up well above the confines of the guardrails.

Coming down, she somehow managed to land on her feet, although she did embarrass herself with a goofy sounding squeal. She gathered her balance and walked over to lean against the guardrail.

"Want to go higher?" he asked with a teasing grin. " 'Cause I'm your man. Just stand right there. I'll send you into space."

"I'm fine right where I am," she said. "Thanks anyway."

The girls clamored for her spot in the center of the contraption. Ezra handled the bickering with an expertise she didn't know he had.

"First time around, we go oldest to youngest."

"I'm first." Chloe grinned, then stuck her tongue out at Amanda. Sophie bit hers to keep from correcting the elder twin.

"Next time," Ezra continued, "we'll go in alphabetical order."

"Then I'm first," Amanda said as she made her way over to the rail to stand by Sophie.

"I like him, Mommy," Amanda said while Chloe was jumping. "He reminds me of Miss Nell."

Sophie patted her daughter's head and smiled. Her thoughts differed from Amanda's. *No, he reminds me of you and Chloe.*

⁂

October 13

For the fourth night in a row, Ezra lay awake well into the night, his mind churning and his heart aching. Had he really been so wrong about Sophie Comeaux and her daughters?

He turned on his side and reached for the journal. The wrapping paper fell to the floor, no doubt sprinkling glitter on the carpet as it had done in Calvin's car and on his clothing after the party.

No matter. This was a gift. If the girls thought glitter was appropriate, then it was.

A strange sensation, this feeling of fondness for people he had only recently met. And yet they felt like family to him, some extension of his grandmother that bridged the gap between her life and her death.

It was all he could do not to get in his car and drop by. Again. If only it weren't so late. Maybe he could bring over popcorn and a movie.

Buck up, Marine. You've got it bad.

Still, those hugs from the girls on Saturday and then again after the trampoline incident were the closest things to heaven he'd experienced in a long time. As much as he hated to admit it, he soaked up their affection like a long-dry sponge.

And Sophie, well, she'd surprised him once again. When would he get used to the fact that seeing her regularly took his breath away?

In his line of work, Ezra saw traitors whose loyalty was purchased by the highest bidder. He'd never understood how a man could go against all he held dear in order to pursue the glittering reward of cold cash or military honor. What he couldn't get out of his mind was that he'd become like those he'd once scorned.

When Sophie Comeaux walked into a room, he became a traitor to his cause and to his grandmother's wishes. What the dark-haired woman didn't know was that, like the mercenaries, Ezra would gladly sell his heart for the glittering reward of a few minutes or hours with her.

Insanity, that's what it was. He'd never felt anything before like this lethal combination of a silly need to impress her and a serious craving to hold her and keep her safe. He desired more time in her presence, and yet he had every reason to despise the person who'd taken advantage of his grandmother.

She claimed she hadn't deceived anyone. The proof would be in the diary, of that he felt certain. Maybe then he could find peace.

He hadn't read Granny Nell's words; there would be time later for that. Rather, he'd held the diary to his chest all the way home, eyes closed. Calvin and Bree surely assumed he was asleep. Only God knew he was praying.

Trouble was, this time his prayers were more unsettling than peaceful. The questions he asked mostly had answers he didn't understand. The few answers he did understand, he didn't like.

Then there was the verse that kept running through his mind. *"For we have no power to face this vast army that is attacking us. We do not know what to do, but our eyes are upon you."*

The words from the last part of verse 12 of 2 Chronicles 20 were written in pen under his cap and engraved on the back of his dog tags. Any other time they would serve as a reminder that no matter what army or enemy he came up against, the Lord stood at his side. Tonight, however, he felt as though they held the warning that his heavenly Father had opted not to climb into the bunker with him for this battle.

All of it combined to send him to bed with an aching head and a troubled heart. When sleep eluded him, Ezra snapped on the light and propped himself up. "Granny Nell, let's see what you have to say."

Ezra opened the journal to the first page and found a familiar accounting of Nell's trip to New Orleans with the senior citizens. They'd gone to an exhibit of the masters only to find the gallery evacuated due to a fire alarm.

In typical Nell Landry fashion, she turned the roadblock into a mere speed bump by convincing the bus driver to take the seniors to another gallery: the shooting gallery at an arcade on Canal Street. There the elderly amused themselves lobbing beanbags at such odd animals as green hippos and purple elephants and taking turns shooting water into little balloon-headed men. By the time the van driver got word that the gallery had reopened, the group was too tired to care and too happy to worry about what they had missed.

" 'Too happy to worry about what we missed.' " Ezra read the words aloud as he closed the book and turned off the light. When was the last time he felt that way?

Tonight on the porch with Sophie, he realized. All evening, in fact.

Ezra groaned. "What's happening, Marine?"

"I don't know, but it certainly will be fun to watch," Calvin said as he appeared in silhouette at the door.

"What are you doing up so late?" Ezra eased into a sitting position and turned on the light. "You usually hit the rack by ten. It's almost midnight."

Calvin affected an irritated look. "Who are you now, my mother?"

"Hey, don't get defensive, pal. I was just kidding."

He said nothing for a moment, then shook his head. "Yeah,

I know. I'm sorry. It's just that I'm a little, well, concerned about something. I've got a possible conflict of interest on a case, and I'm not sure how to handle it."

"Really? Which case?"

"Yours."

twenty-five

"Mine?"

He nodded. "I'm afraid so."

"What's the problem?" Ezra snapped his fingers and pointed at Calvin. "Bree Jackson. She's the conflict, isn't she?"

Calvin's expression was purposefully vague. "What makes you think that?"

"Oh, I don't know. Didn't I hear you making plans on the phone to drive out and see her after work tomorrow?"

Vague turned into defensive, and Calvin stuffed his fists into his jeans pockets. "You make it sound like I'm dating the woman. It so happens her car is still making that strange noise. I'm merely going to see if I can assist her."

"I see." Ezra pounded his pillows, then fell into them. "Doesn't sound like you've got a conflict at all."

His friend smiled. "You don't think so?"

"Nah," Ezra said. "Sounds like you two are getting along real well."

"Oh, very funny." He paused. "Look who's talking, Ezra. I saw you on the porch with Sophie Comeaux. If I hadn't honked the horn, you probably would have kissed her."

"I doubt that." But did he really believe what he'd just said? He couldn't deny the thought crossed his mind while he was standing there in the moonlight.

Calvin still stood in the doorway. The poor guy looked miserable.

"Okay, so maybe Miss Jackson ought to call AAA and get her car towed to a repair shop," Ezra said. "I mean, you are going against her in a lawsuit. It wouldn't be right to fraternize with the enemy."

"Look—all kidding aside." Calvin lowered himself into the

141

chair and propped his feet on the ottoman. "How serious are you about going forward with this lawsuit?"

"I don't know." Ezra raked his hands through his hair. "Okay, so maybe I have had a couple of things happen that make me wonder."

"Like gardening and trampoline jumping?"

Ezra cringed. "You heard."

"Bree might have mentioned it last night."

He sighed. "Anyway, you know I'm up for that job in the Pentagon, right?"

"I remember you telling me about it when the general called. You really thinking of leaving special ops? I figured you'd be chasing bad guys through the desert in your wheelchair before you'd quit."

"There's something to be said for getting out while I'm still at the top of my game." Ezra sighed. "Working national security would pretty much be the same job, except I don't have to sleep in a tent and eat bugs for dinner. And then there's the promotion. I've waited all my career to reach the rank of lieutenant colonel."

Calvin made a face. "You ate bugs? What kind?"

"Crunchy ones, and only a couple of times. Tasted just like chicken." He paused to chuckle. "Anyway, in your opinion as my attorney, what would it hurt to put this off for a while and let Sophie and the girls live there? I don't mean permanently. Just while I'm in D.C."

Calvin sat up a little straighter. "Go on."

"Yeah, well, the general's going to make his decision any day now, which means I don't have the time to dispose of the property and Granny Nell's things." Ezra shrugged. "I don't want to rush into anything."

"Let me see if I am hearing you correctly. You're saying you want to nonsuit the case and lease the house to the Comeaux family?"

"If *nonsuit* means we don't go to court next month, that's what I want."

"Will Sophie go for the lease idea?"

Ezra shrugged. "Only one way to find out. We're meeting tomorrow to work on the Founders' Day thing. I'll see what she says and let you know."

◆

October 14

Sophie arranged the photo albums on the coffee table, then made a space for the tray of coffee and cookies. An arrangement of camellias from the front yard and two cloth napkins folded in the shape of a fan completed the tabletop setting.

"Perfect." She took two steps back and frowned. "Too perfect. He'll think I'm an idiot."

Setting everything but the photo albums back on the tray, she returned to the kitchen. "If he wants coffee or something to eat, he can ask." She placed the tray on the counter and reached for the apple cookie jar. "Wait—that's not very nice. Maybe I can put the things on the kitchen table. Then he'll know they're there."

Sophie tossed the napkins onto the counter and groaned. "What's wrong with me? I'm acting like this is some sort of date. We are just two people who happen to care about the same person and want to work together to honor that person."

Yeah, right. She set the cookie jar's lid aside and began to pour the cookies back into it.

The doorbell rang, and Sophie jumped. Cookies tumbled to the counter, and crumbs littered the tray and decorated the bottoms of the coffee cups. *Great.*

Sophie snagged the dishrag and mopped the crumbs into the tray, then set it inside the oven. "Coming," she called as the doorbell rang a second time.

She paused at the mirror beside the door to check her hair, then froze. "What am I doing? I don't even like this man."

But as she said the words, she knew they weren't the complete truth. While she didn't like his idea of how to handle the issue of the house, she found Ezra, well, interesting. The girls certainly liked him.

If only he weren't a marine. And trying to evict her.

Ding-dong.

Sophie reached to open the door, setting her smile in place as she turned the knob. "Hey," she said. "Sorry about the delay. Come in."

Why hadn't she noticed before what a lovely smile the man had?

Ezra brushed past her to deposit a box on the table beside the albums. "Miss Emmeline sent a few things that might get us started."

He opened the lid to reveal a hodgepodge of papers and photographs. Topmost was a photograph of an older couple and a somewhat sullen-looking young man standing in front of the Riverside house. In the foreground was a red bicycle with high handlebars and a banana seat.

Sophie picked up the picture and turned it over. "Robbie Junior's thirteenth birthday." She handed the photograph to Ezra. "Who is Robbie Junior?"

"Me. That was my name before the Landrys adopted me. See, technically Nell and the reverend were my adoptive parents. Because she was so much older, I just took to calling her Granny Nell like the others she took in. I'd already had a mom and. . ." He tossed the picture back into the box and set the lid atop it. "Look—I've said too much. Maybe this wasn't such a good idea."

Sophie rested her hand on his. "I understand."

Ezra jerked his hand away and rose, his face a mask of conflicting emotions. "You have no idea."

"I'm sorry," she said quickly. "Of course I don't. It was a stupid thing to say."

He paced to the door, then returned to join her on the sofa. "I'm sorry. I shouldn't have snapped at you. It's just that, well, some memories are best left alone."

She thought of her near wedding. "I agree."

He looked surprised. "You do?"

"Sure." She pushed the box out of the way and reached for her notepad. "Maybe we ought to concentrate on something more pleasant, like what we would like to say about Nell."

Settling into the sofa cushions, Ezra smiled. "I like that idea."

Pen poised, Sophie looked to Ezra to begin dictating. He said nothing.

"Ezra?" She pointed to the paper with her pen. "What's the first thing that comes to mind when I ask you to tell me who Nell was?"

"Car keys."

"What?"

"The first thing that comes to mind is that it would be easier to show you who Nell was than to tell you. And for that I would need the car keys."

Sophie checked her watch. "I have two hours before the girls get home. Will this take long?"

Ezra grinned, and her heart did that goofy flip-flop again. This time not even the reminder that he was not a man in whom she should take an interest worked. *Lord, please help me to stop this silliness.*

And yet when she looked at Ezra, she imagined a man with a past he didn't like and a future yet to be lived. A man whom her girls adored and she had somehow developed an attraction to. It was silly but true. She was glad she would never have to worry about whether her feelings were reciprocated. They wouldn't be.

"I think I can give you the two-hour tour."

Sophie grabbed her purse and followed Ezra toward the door. Without warning he stopped, and she slammed into his chest. Stunned, she couldn't quite feature what had happened. Then she looked up into dark eyes, felt strong arms holding her, and gasped.

twenty-six

"Oh. . .I'm. . .sorry."

She took a step backward and collided with the wall, dislodging a picture of the girls. Ezra caught it before it hit the ground and set it on the table.

"No, I'm sorry, Sophie," Ezra said. He shook his head. "I just thought I should warn you to wear shoes you don't mind getting dirty. We're going to do some walking, a lot of it around the bayou."

She looked down at her leather shoes and frowned. "Give me a second, and I'll change."

Somehow she made her way back to her room without crashing into anything. Once inside the safe confines, she sank onto her bed and covered her face with her hands.

"He thinks I'm an idiot," she whispered.

After composing herself and taking a quick peek in the bathroom mirror, she slipped on walking shoes and headed for the door. Sophie found Ezra staring at the picture she'd knocked from the wall. He looked upset again.

"Something wrong?"

Ezra set the picture on the table and turned his attention to Sophie. "Just looking at the girls. They're very pretty."

"They are."

"I don't know how much you find out about birth parents these days, but I wonder if they are originally from Latagnier. Something about them looks familiar. Maybe I know the mom or dad."

He opened the door for Sophie, then followed her outside.

"I have the birth parents' names, but I didn't think to look at where they were born," she said as she fitted the key into the lock. "I was just happy to get them, you know?"

"Yes." He helped her into the car, then jogged around to get into the driver's seat and crank the engine. "All right, Sophie, I'm going to take you on a tour."

Silence fell between them as Ezra guided the car onto Main Street, then turned at the old highway at the edge of Latagnier. In a matter of minutes, the city fell away, and the lush bayou country beckoned. The chilly October temperatures had turned the green countryside into a forest of burnt oranges and browns.

Ezra drove with his window slightly cracked, allowing the scent of freshly plowed cane fields to permeate the car. "Louisiana is a different sort of place, Sophie. There's something here that you just can't find anywhere else."

She leaned against the door and felt the handle jab into her arm. "What's that?"

He looked at her before he spoke, fixing his gaze on her for a moment longer than felt comfortable to her. "Family, I guess, and history, several centuries of both. But then you know the story of the Acadians, and I'm sure you know how we Cajuns are about family."

"Yes, I do." She smiled. "But only from textbooks. I don't know what that kind of family lineage is like. All I have is my great-aunt Alta who lives in Tulsa."

He slowed to turn left, then gave her an incredulous look. "So you've never experienced the fun of having more than thirty relatives all trying to eat from the same turkey at Thanksgiving? Never spent Christmas Eve with seventy-three of your closest relatives?"

She shook her head and suppressed a giggle.

"Poor girl. You haven't lived."

If only he knew how his words hit the mark. Somehow her pitiful efforts to make the holidays joyous and festive with just the three of them in attendance seemed a bit sad.

He must have sensed her change of mood, for he pulled the car to the side of the road at a rest stop near the bayou and shifted into PARK. "Hey, I put my big foot in my mouth, didn't I?"

Sophie tried to make light of the statement by looking down at his feet. "Oh, I don't know. That doesn't seem possible."

"Look—I don't know anything about you, and you probably don't know a whole lot about me. Outside of this stuff about the house, I think, well. . ." Ezra studied the steering wheel, then watched the taillights of the eighteen-wheeler as it screamed past. "I think you're someone I would have liked to get to know."

"Me, too," she said softly. Then she giggled. "I sound like Amanda."

Ezra swiveled to face her. "Just so you know, I really have taken a liking to your girls. Maybe it's because my grandmother cared for them so much, but they feel like family." He met her stare, and a nerve in his cheek twitched.

"I know they've been happy to know you. I think your coming here when you did was God's way of helping the girls get over Miss Nell's death. Until you came, they didn't talk about her the way they do now. In fact, they didn't talk about her at all."

"Yeah, me, too." His attention darted to Sophie. "Now I sound like Amanda." They shared a laugh as Ezra pulled back onto the road. "We're almost there."

"Where are we going?"

"First the Latagnier School and then a walk down Bayou Nouvelle to the old Trahan place. Are you game?"

"Definitely."

A few minutes later, Ezra turned off the main road onto a narrow dirt lane bound by a cane field to the right and thick trees on the left. Up ahead the road made a sharp turn to the left, and just beyond that, a white frame house came into view. The vintage was new according to bayou standards, probably 1970s.

As they passed, Ezra gestured to the one-story home. "My best friend lived there. He was a Lamont. Kin to the Breaux family through marriage, so we were distant cousins. They built this place when the old homestead was leveled in Camille." He shrugged. "Sorry, I sound like Miss Emmeline."

Sophie smiled. "Don't apologize. I like it."

"You do? Well now," he said as he glanced over at her and grinned, "I'll have to throw in more history. It pleases the lady."

"Yes," she said softly, "it does. Say, what's that?"

Ezra pointed toward the horizon where a ramshackle cabin stood in a clearing. "That is Latagnier's first school. Back then it sat on the property of Joe Trahan, kin to Miss Emmeline. Nowadays it's owned by the city of Latagnier. Someday it will be a museum or something; leastwise that's what the talk was a few years ago."

He pulled the car to a stop and turned off the engine. "Ready?"

"Sure," she said as she climbed out of the car.

They walked across the clearing and up to the structure. Made of cypress wood, it was designed in the old Acadian way with a center stair going up from the outside and a porch that ran the length of the front. Sophie could imagine turn-of-the-century children playing in the clearing and racing to desks when the teacher rang the bell.

"This is where my grandmother went to school." He ran his fingers over the rail and smiled. "Whoever built this meant for it to last."

Sophie tried to keep her attention on the building, but she found it wandering to her guide. When he caught her looking, she pretended interest in the window behind him. "Why is it boarded up?"

"Hurricane proofing, I guess." He paused to test the structural integrity of the porch, then gestured toward the door. "Want to go inside?"

"Can we?"

He nodded. "Stick close to me. With these windows boarded up, it could be dark in there."

Only one board stood between them and entry to the building, and Ezra made short work of it. Sophie watched as he lifted the lumber over his head and tossed it into the yard as if it were a child's toy.

Pushing on the door didn't work, so he gave it a sharp kick. The ancient wood swung open on loud hinges, and the musty scent of sawdust and many years of disuse billowed out.

"I'll go first. Give me your hand."

Sophie slipped her hand in his and took a deep breath, which she instantly regretted. She began to cough, sputtering like a fool in front of the man whose hand she held.

Ezra reached into his pocket and handed her a handkerchief. "Here, put this over your mouth so the dust won't bother you." When he saw her reluctance, he grinned. "It's clean. I promise."

Sophie complied, and instantly she breathed easier. The handkerchief smelled like soap and Ezra's aftershave. The combination was lovely. "Thank you."

"Ready?"

When she nodded, he led her into a large room bathed in stripes of sunlight and shadows and filled with stacks of what looked like small wooden desks. Even through the handkerchief, the musty smell lingered. She blinked hard to adjust her eyes to the dimness. Slowly, items came into focus.

"What was this room used for?"

"It's the old schoolroom. As many times as I've been in here, I never was able to imagine my grandmother in one of those desks."

"How many times have you been in here, Ezra?"

"More than I ought to have, that's for sure." He ducked his head. "In my former life I wasn't such a sterling character."

She squeezed his hand. "I find that hard to believe."

"Well then, I won't tell you I learned to chew tobacco back behind this building, and I loved to bring girls out here and scare them with ghost stories."

"So they would cuddle up to you, no doubt."

"No doubt." He looked down with a broad grin. "For the record, I've given up both of those bad habits."

Something scurried across the floor, and Sophie screamed. She leaned into Ezra and felt his arm going around her.

"It's all right." Ezra released his embrace to point to the windowsill. "It's a squirrel."

Sophie gave him a sideways look as she waited for her heart to slow its frantic pace. "I have to say that was suspicious timing. Do you happen to have a squirrel on your payroll, Major Landry?"

He chuckled. "No, but it's beginning to sound like a good idea."

For a moment neither moved. Then Ezra cleared his throat. "Well, I guess that's about all there is to see here. I just wanted to give you an idea of something from my grandmother's past."

Ezra led her outside where she reluctantly released her grip and returned the handkerchief. The sunlight burned her eyes, and she blinked.

"Now how about that walk I promised?" He pointed to a spot behind the cabin. "The bayou's that way."

She fell into step beside Ezra. "The ground we're walking on used to belong to my grandmother's parents. They bought a sliver of the Breaux property just after the Depression and built a house on it."

"What happened to the house?"

"It was sold after they died. Do you know that story?"

When Sophie shook her head, Ezra gestured to a fallen log. "Let's go sit for a minute, and I'll tell you how my grandmother came to be an orphan."

twenty-seven

"And so she stayed at the Buckner Home in Dallas until she was of age. That's when she left with her brother—my dad—and came back to Latagnier to work at the church."

Ezra paused in his tale to gauge the mood of his guest. She seemed interested enough. Still, better not to overdo the family stuff. His mention of the holidays seemed to set her in a blue mood.

They sat side by side on the log, near enough to nudge but far enough away to keep his attention focused on something—anything—but her.

"You tell that story much better than Miss Emmeline." Sophie seemed to be thinking hard about something. "May I ask you a question?"

"Sure."

"What happened to your father?"

What to tell her? The truth or a carefully stated substitute?

"He's not a part of my life anymore. Miss Emmeline was right when she said he came home from the war a different man."

"I'm sorry," she said as she touched his hand.

"Sophie, I think we need to walk now." He rose and grasped her hand. "Let me show you the Bayou Nouvelle."

She came along at his pace, which was nice of her considering he tended to walk briskly. Occasionally he would slow down only to have her pass him up. When they reached the bayou, she slipped her hand from his and picked her way down to the water.

"There's a family story that tells how a gator once pursued old Doc Villare, and one of the Breaux girls got chased up that tree over there."

Sophie giggled. "You're kidding, right?"

"Nope. Hey, want to see Granddaddy's church?"

"Sure."

"It's that way. We can follow the path that runs along the bayou."

The sun warmed Ezra's back as he walked alongside Sophie. *Ah, Sophie.* Now there was a problem in need of solving.

Although he'd only known her a short while, he felt as if the Lord was urging him to include her in his future plans. The idea had scared him when it first came to him, and nothing scared Major Ezra Landry. Well, not the old Ezra. Something about Sophie and the girls had changed him.

He needed to tell her. "So, Sophie, there's something I've been wanting to—"

"What's that?" She walked over to the bayou's edge and pointed at the black water.

Ezra sidled up beside her and looked in the general direction where she pointed. "You mean that gar?"

"If a gar is a giant fish that looks like something out of the dinosaur age, then yes."

He chuckled. "Yes, that's a gar. They're nasty looking but generally harmless unless provoked. Like me," he added.

She turned to face him. "I disagree."

Now that came out of nowhere. "You do?"

She nodded. "You don't look the least bit nasty. In fact, for a marine you're quite handsome."

Sophie gave him that what-have-I-said look, then turned and continued walking toward the church. He'd never seen her flirt before, and he liked it.

"There's the church. See the steeple?"

"Yes, I see it."

She picked up her pace, and he fell in step. Soon they reached the churchyard. A wood-framed church sat in the center of the clearing. Painted a brilliant white, the tall steeple punctuated the blue sky. A pair of stained glass windows flanked the double wooden doors. It was the picture of nostalgic simplicity.

"They still use the place sometimes. It's popular for weddings."

"Oh." She walked around to the side, then down past the graveyard to the giant Easter cross.

"That cross was built by two of the Breaux boys some hundred years ago, give or take."

Sophie ran her hand over the smooth wood, then touched her flattened palms to it. "It's lovely," she said softly. "Just lovely."

"Yes," he said as he drew near. *Too near.* "You are."

She looked up at him, shock registering. "What did you say?"

Ezra stared into her eyes. "I said you're beautiful."

"Oh."

The wind blew cold on the back of his neck. "Is that all you can say?"

"Thank you?"

He leaned closer. "I was hoping for more enthusiasm."

Sophie caught a soft breath. "Ezra, this is awkward."

Taking two steps back, he began apologizing. What an idiot he'd been. "You're right. We should go," he added as he turned to head toward the car.

Catching his arm, Sophie dragged him around to face her. "No, you don't get it. The awkward thing is, I like you, Ezra. I was enjoying your attention."

"You were?" Ezra barely suppressed a smile. "What's awkward about that?"

She shrugged. "Ancient history and present-day lawsuits."

"Yeah," he said slowly as he captured her in his arms, "about that lawsuit. I talked to Calvin yesterday. See, there's this thing called a nonsuit. That's where. . .oh, Sophie, I'm going to kiss you now and tell you about how I'm dropping the suit later, okay?"

"Okay" drifted to him as a soft whisper.

The kiss was all he hoped and all he dreaded. Why God led him to Sophie Comeaux was beyond understanding, and yet in the brief moment of that kiss, he felt the Lord had fashioned him to stand in that spot and kiss that girl. It was a clarity of purpose he'd only experienced once before when he joined the Marine Corps.

"Ezra, what does this mean?"

A direct woman. I like that.

"Well, Sophie, it means that you and I are going to see where the Lord wants this to go." He lifted her chin with his forefinger and kissed her nose. "Is that okay with you?"

She nodded. "But this is so fast. So unexpected. I mean, when I invited you to the barbecue, I wanted to dislike you. I really intended to show you just what a creep you were." She lifted her gaze to him, and he noticed for the first time that her eyes were a soft moss green. "I'm sorry."

"Oh, honey, no. I *was* a creep." He mustered a smile. "Still am on occasion. It's one of my spiritual gifts." Holding up his hands, he chuckled. "I'm kidding."

They walked back in silence, arms linked. Ezra knew he'd never spent a better afternoon. He just hoped he didn't regret admitting his feelings to Sophie. After all, he'd never found time for long-term relationships. The fact that the Lord might be calling him to that with Sophie gave him pause.

I'll learn if You'll teach me.

When they reached the car, Ezra opened the door for Sophie, but she did not step inside. Rather, she reached for the fabric of his shirt and gave him a pleading look. "This is crazy, Ezra. You know that, right?"

"What do you mean?"

"We barely know one another, and we met under less-than-favorable circumstances."

He gathered her into an embrace, one that was beginning to feel like going home. "Sophie, not everything God does makes sense. I think He, and probably my grandmother, intended for us to find one another."

"I'm going to need time to get used to this, Ezra. I don't know if I can be in a relationship again."

Ezra looked into her eyes. "Sophie, when you're ready to tell me about 'again,' I will be ready to listen. In the meantime, let's just see where the Lord leads."

She nodded and climbed in the car. Ezra shut the door and walked around to drive them back to Riverside Avenue. They rode in silence, fingers entwined, until Ezra pulled into the driveway.

"Fifteen minutes to spare." He went around to open Sophie's door and help her out. "I guess we didn't get much done today."

"I don't know. I learned a lot about your grandmother." She lifted her gaze to collide with his. "And about you."

Ezra smiled. "There's one thing I'd like to do before the girls get home. I wonder if you'd come with me to my grandmother's side of the house. I want to say good-bye to her."

They walked up the steps together, but Sophie hung back and let him approach the door alone.

"Buck up, Marine," he whispered as he jammed the key into position and forced himself to open the door.

Although he'd come over to fetch the cookie jar before, he'd rushed in and out of the house as quickly as possible. This time would be different.

The door slid open on silent hinges, revealing the immaculate entry hall. Half the size he remembered, the room still unfolded on a comfortable scale with a polished hardwood floor covered in a scattering of rugs. Beyond it lay the dining room where an oval rosewood table stood waiting for Nell to cover it with dishes of country ham, black-eyed peas, and bread pudding.

His ears echoed with the last conversation he'd had with Nell across this very same table, and his mouth still tasted the sweet dessert and coffee as well as the bitter words.

All the things he'd meant to say and didn't, the things he'd planned to say but couldn't came flooding back. In his mind, Nell sat in her place across from him, the large-print Bible she cherished in her lap and her fingers sliding across the page as she read aloud from the scriptures.

"I miss you, Granny Nell," he whispered to the image as it faded, the singsong chant of girls at play outside breaking the spell.

Dropping his key on the flowered carpet beside the staircase, Ezra took a few slow steps into the room. Many years of memories assailed him, each of them equally wonderful and sadly dusty with lack of use.

In an instant the silence engulfed him. And then he heard Nell's voice. "A father to the fatherless, a defender of widows, is God in his holy dwelling."

He paused to touch the banister, then recoiled from the smooth wood as if he'd been burned. Nothing about this empty house felt right.

Turning on his heels, he strode to the door. Stopping just short, Ezra turned to say one last good-bye to Granny Nell, to his former life, and to the home his granny called her dwelling place.

Sophie waited on the porch, and he fell into her arms and sobbed like a baby. She held him tight until the feelings passed, then pointed to his pocket. "Use your handkerchief. Hey, it's clean. I promise."

He blew his nose, then chuckled despite himself.

Sophie touched his arm. "Ezra, I want you to know something. You can have the house. I'll ask for more hours at the hospital. I can find another place."

Ezra silenced her with his forefinger to her lips. "Don't, Sophie. You and the girls aren't going anywhere. My grandmother will have to understand."

"I know in my heart this is what she intended to happen, Ezra. Thank you. And I know the girls will be pleased. This is the only home they've really known."

Ezra waited for the regret, but it refused to arrive. No, he felt good, very good.

He felt as if he'd come home.

twenty-eight

October 25

Ezra read the report for the third time, hoping to keep his mind on what was contained on the page. As with the previous two attempts, it did not work.

Thoughts of Sophie Comeaux pushed away any other rational considerations, a dangerous thing when a classified brief sat unread. For the past two weeks, most of his waking moments had been spent either thinking of her or being in her presence. He'd thus far acted the close friend, with no more stolen kisses, but each time he saw her, that persona cracked a bit more.

Going to the Lord with his dilemma worked fine this time. He felt a real peace at what was happening with Sophie. Funny, but he hadn't known any sort of peace in ages, not since Granny Nell.

This morning in his quiet time, the Lord spoke as clear as day. Sophie was *the one.* Now all he had to do was figure out how to tell her that.

He picked up his cell phone and punched in her number, thinking he might speak to her for just a moment and slake his thirst. The phone rang three times; then her voice mail picked up.

"Just thinking of tonight," he said. "I hope you're working hard on your speech for Founders' Day."

He smiled as he hung up. That last part would get her good. The one thing they'd managed to decide was that she would write the speech about Granny Nell, and he would give it.

Miss Emmeline had changed her mind about a presentation, preferring a simple ceremony instead. "That's what

Nell would have wanted," was her explanation. Ezra agreed, as did Sophie.

He looked up at the clock. A quarter to two. He got off at five. With time to change and the drive over, he could be there with pizza and a movie by six. The girls would love that. He'd have to find out what movie to get, but that shouldn't be too difficult. Sophie was a good mom. She seemed to have all the answers to questions of that nature.

Ezra rose. Maybe he would slip out early and see if Sophie was on her way to pick up the girls. It was Tuesday, and he thought that could be the day she drove them home rather than picked them up from day care.

Pulling his keys from his pocket, Ezra headed for the door. If he hurried, maybe he could ride along to pick up the girls. It would be interesting to see where they went to school. Maybe he could even help them with their homework.

He stopped cold. "What am I doing thinking about second-grade homework and elementary school car pools? I've got it bad."

"Yeah, I noticed." Calvin stood in the door studying him. "Leaving early? It's not five yet."

"Yeah, I've got some things to do."

"Things like go see Sophie and the girls?"

Ezra studied the keys in his hand. "Maybe.

"Well, now that you've signed the order of nonsuit, I feel free to tell you two things. First, I heartily approve of your spending time at the Riverside Avenue home. Sophie is wonderful, and her girls are very well behaved." He paused. "Second, I'm going to ask Bree to marry me."

"What?" Ezra shook his head. "Are you kidding me? You've only known her, what, three weeks?"

"Yeah, I know, and it's a little hard for me to fathom, too. It's just that I can't get her out of my mind. When I try to concentrate on a case, she's all I think of, and when I am away from her, I am plotting a way to get to see her. I expect a long engagement, though, a year to eighteen months probably.

We might have rushed into love, but we won't rush into marriage."

Ezra exhaled a long breath. "Yeah, I hear you."

Calvin gave him a sideways glance. "You feeling that way, too, Green Beret?"

"Guilty," he said. "But unlike you I'm not so sure marrying her is the right thing to do. I mean, I've got a career going here, and I don't want to mess it up."

"And a louse of a father to prove something to."

"Okay. Sure, that's a consideration. But what if I am called to duty elsewhere? What will happen?"

"She'd go with you, Ezra. Stop making things so complicated." He paused. "Have you heard anything from the Pentagon?"

He shook his head. "Every time the phone rings, I jump."

"Want my advice?"

"As my lawyer or my friend?"

Calvin chuckled. "Both. Remember, it doesn't matter what honor you receive from men; the only true rank is the one the Lord bestows on us. When you're in His will, nothing else matters."

"You're right, Cal," Ezra said. "You must have gotten that smart hanging around with me."

"Yeah, right, and if I keep hanging around with you instead of doing my job, they'll bust me back to private."

"All right then. See you later. I'm heading out." He reached for his briefcase, and the phone rang. "This is Major Landry."

"Hello, Major Landry. Barnes here."

Brigadier General Stenson Barnes, chief of operations at the Pentagon's Marine Security Division. Ezra gulped and gripped the phone.

"Yes, sir. Hello, sir."

"Pleasantries aside, I want to tell you that our office needs a man like you. Pay's much better than the money Scanlon could offer, and I'm bumping you up to lieutenant colonel. I'll need you here November 1. Any questions?"

He sank into his chair. "Well, sir, I—"

"Good. My assistant will fax over the particulars. Congratulations, son."

Click.

Ezra stared at the phone until it set off a warning recording. Easing the receiver back onto the cradle, he stared at the contraption until he remembered to blink.

There it was, everything he wanted all laid out nice and pretty. He'd met his father's expectations and matched his rank. Another few years and he'd beat him. The satisfaction in that was immeasurable.

How could he turn the job down? And yet how could he leave now?

Ezra leaned back, and the chair protested. What was wrong with him?

Getting too close, that's what was wrong. He'd chosen to fall in love. No, that choice had been taken out of his hands. Love had happened when he wasn't looking; he'd only been a willing participant.

Love. He swallowed hard.

Unfortunately a man in his position didn't have a place in his life for love. The job would take all he had, leaving nothing in the way of time or, most likely, emotion for anyone else. And then there was the travel. No, a man couldn't burden a wife and kids with that sort of abandonment.

He couldn't go, and yet he had to take the job. There was no other choice.

Ezra felt no peace in his heart about the decision, but he had no time to wait to see what he should do. He had to act.

"Buck up, Marine. She'll understand."

❧

It might be October, but Sophie's garden looked like spring would come any moment. The rows were nice and straight, and no weeds were to be found. Thanks to Ezra and the girls, they would have plenty of fresh vegetables next year.

What a treat.

The chilly air combined with the brilliant afternoon sun made for pleasant conditions in the backyard. If she didn't have so much to do, she might consider jumping on the trampoline. What fun that had been.

"Sophie, are you back there?"

"Yes, I'm in the garden, Ezra." She rose and dusted off her gloves, then let them drop in the grass. As he rounded the corner, she smiled. "I was just thinking about you."

He strode over to her and kissed her soundly. When he released her, she smiled.

"Wow! What was that for?"

"Sit down, Sophie."

She followed him to the porch steps and settled beside him.

"There's really no good way to tell you this, so I'll just come right out and say I'm leaving."

Sophie blinked hard. "Leaving? Where are you going?"

"Remember the Pentagon job I told you about?" He waited for her to nod. "Well, I got it and a raise in pay and rank."

Last Sunday after church he'd told her of his strained relationship with his father and the fact that he owed his military career to the drive he'd instilled to best the man who gave him away. In turn she told him about First Lieutenant Jim Hebert and the Lake Charles wedding that wasn't.

She'd been slightly concerned about opening her heart to him then, but now she was terrified. Another man was walking away.

"What about Founders' Day?" was the only thing she could think of to say.

Ezra gathered her into his arms and rested his chin on her head. "Sophie, I've got to report on November 1."

Sophie buried her face in his shirt and fought tears. "That's only a week away." She pulled away to look up into coffee-colored eyes. "Would you stay if I told you I loved you?"

His silence spoke volumes.

She rose and walked in the house without a word.

twenty-nine

Sophie stabbed at the garden, not caring what the shovel hit. Digging in the dirt was the only thing that satisfied the need to do something—anything—about the feelings raging inside her. Ezra had left three days ago, and he'd called several dozen times since. She listened to his messages but thus far hadn't been able to bring herself to answer the phone.

She heard Bree's car pull up. "Get it together, Sophie," she whispered. "You don't want the girls to see you like this."

Bree waved, and the dazzling rock on her left hand nearly blinded Sophie. The little dog in her arms, a gift from Calvin, barked.

"Back from the park so soon?"

Bree shrugged. "The puppy's little. I was afraid she was getting cold."

"Honey, she's wearing her fur coat and that silly one you bought her, too. I'm sure she's warm enough." Sophie looked past Bree to the garden gate. "Where's Calvin?"

"He went home. I told him I wanted to speak to you privately."

"Uh-oh. Here comes another lecture."

Bree set the white dust mop of a dog on the ground, then shook her head. "I am not going to lecture. I merely intended to point out that you and Ezra seem to be made for one another. I just think this separation is something God can work with. Maybe it's supposed to show him how much he needs you and the girls."

"Well, maybe so." Sophie stabbed the shovel into the dirt, then leaned on it. "But if He is so keen on working this out for us, why isn't He bringing Ezra back? You know why he left, don't you? About his father?"

163

"Calvin shared a little bit about that. Just that he left Ezra as a young teen, and Ezra's felt a need to prove himself to the guy ever since."

"Yes, well, Ezra is out proving a point to someone who doesn't care, and I'm here feeling like I was left at the altar again. It's crazy, I know, because he never told me he loved me, but I thought. . ." Tears threatened, and Sophie swiped at them with her sleeve. "I'm sorry, Bree. This is a happy time for you. You certainly don't need to listen to my complaining."

Bree picked up the puppy and began to scratch his ears. "You're not complaining, Soph. And you have every right to be upset."

"I just wanted this to work out, you know? I mean, it's only been a short while, but I thought Ezra was the one. It was nothing like the first time around back in Lake Charles. I even got past the fact that Ezra was a marine, too. This really felt like God was behind it. And the way he was with the girls—oh, Bree, it was as if they were his own flesh and blood."

"I liked that about him," she said softly. "He treated Amanda and Chloe so well."

Sophie met her friend's gaze. "Can I admit something to you? I told him I loved him. Well, in a roundabout way. I asked him if my saying I loved him would be enough to keep him here." She sniffed and wiped her eyes with her sleeve again. "It didn't."

"Maybe not, but you have to believe it will be enough to bring him back." Bree set the dog down again, then embraced Sophie. "Honey, I think God is behind all this. It's just that sometimes people have to go to all sorts of trouble proving themselves before they figure out they've got nothing to prove." She held Sophie out at arm's length. "Change of topic. Tell me what you have written for the Founders' Day speech."

"It's inside. Let's go in for coffee, and I'll let you see what you think." Sophie dried her eyes and gave her friend a hug. "Thank you for helping me by speaking on Founders' Day, Bree. I just couldn't have, especially now."

She shrugged. "It was nothing. I do this all the time in court, remember? At least this time I don't have to worry which way the jury will vote."

≈

November 16

Founders' Day dawned cold and clear. Ice dusted Sophie's windshield, very much like the layer her heart wore.

She'd written and rewritten the speech honoring Nell Landry until she could say it in her sleep. Now all that remained was to listen to Bree read it.

If only Ezra were there. He should be in attendance today. A nagging thought pricked at her conscience. *If only you'd answered the phone when he called.*

She shifted positions and pushed her doubts away. No, she'd done the right thing. When a man leaves, you let him go.

Somewhere along the tenth or eleventh day after he left, Ezra finally stopped calling. Sophie didn't know whether to be offended or relieved. Her current state of numbness wouldn't allow her to make the decision.

The parade complete, Sophie sat in the front row of the high school auditorium and waited for Bree to emerge from behind the red, white, and blue curtain Miss Emmeline had fashioned to hide the plaque from view. To Sophie's mind, the contraption looked more like a patriotic voting booth.

Chloe had borrowed a pen and was drawing flowers all over the program while Amanda leaned against Sophie's arm, her eyes half closed. Someone coughed; then the stage lights went up, and the high school band played a patriotic song.

When the music ended, Miss Emmeline stepped up to the microphone and tapped it. The resulting squeal made Sophie cringe. The girls stuck their fingers in their ears and made faces until it stopped.

"Ladies and gentlemen, our first-ever honoree. . ."

Sophie let her mind wander as Miss Emmeline began to describe Nell. Her dear friend might have complained about all the fuss, but in her heart Sophie felt Nell would be pleased.

Miss Emmeline had showed her the plaque yesterday. Under a picture of Nell taken in her prime was the fifth verse from Psalm 68: *A father to the fatherless, a defender of widows, is God in his holy dwelling.* Following the verse was a simple tribute to the woman who'd loved so many:

> *Nell Landry lived her life in service to others, especially those orphaned by chance or choice. In her life she brought orphans into families and shone the light of the Lord into a dark world. She will be remembered as the mother of many and the defender of all who searched for a dwelling place.*

Miss Emmeline wound down her speech, then looked over at Sophie. "The people of Latagnier honor her today as the woman who was always ready to offer love and comfort to a neighbor or an orphan. Miss Sophie Comeaux, Nell's dear friend, has written a tribute that Miss Bree Jackson was to have read to you. Instead you will find the tribute framed beside the plaque at city hall."

Out of the corner of her eye, Sophie caught sight of Bree coming toward them to sit beside Chloe. "What's going on?" she asked Bree.

"Pay attention," Bree said as Calvin appeared through the crowd and took the seat next to her. "You, too, girls."

Miss Emmeline continued. "If I have your permission, Sophie, I would like to introduce someone else who will read a portion of what you wrote, along with some personal comments."

The curtains parted, and out stepped Ezra in full dress uniform holding the bronze plaque. His back ramrod straight, he marched to the easel and placed his grandmother's award on it, then took a moment to stand at attention before it.

He looked to be praying, and Sophie felt the tears gather. Until she saw Ezra, Sophie hadn't admitted to herself how much she missed him. He gave a salute, then turned on his heels to make his way to the podium.

The microphone was far too low for a man of his height, so Ezra had to lean forward to be heard. He greeted the crowd, then looked over at Sophie and the girls. "I want to read something that someone very special wrote about Nell Landry, my father's sister and the woman who raised me."

Tears glittered and blurred the stage until Bree handed Sophie a handkerchief. It smelled of Nell's favorite perfume, which made her cry harder.

"There is a point in our lives where God takes us by the hand and asks us the hard questions," Ezra read aloud. "We all must answer those questions. When God asked Nell if she understood that sometimes being a mother means mothering others whose lives you did not create, I believe she answered with a hearty, 'Yes.'"

Ezra set down the page and paused. "I know there are many people present today whose lives were touched by Nell Landry. Many of you lived in her home. She loved her work with the orphans, so some of you may have been blessed by knowing her through the state children's home. By a show of hands, how many of you found families because Nell Landry took an interest in you and matched you up with friends or family willing to welcome you in?"

Sophie looked around the auditorium, astounded at the number of hands raised. Then she looked down at her own girls and saw they, too, had their hands in the air. Onstage, Ezra had set the paper down and now held his hand high.

Smiling, Sophie, too, held up her hand. If she hadn't met Nell, she would never have been part of a family. She might not be an orphan in the conventional sense, but she qualified as one of Miss Nell's success stories all the same.

"That is the legacy of a woman of God," Ezra continued. "And it shows how one person can make a difference. I challenge you all to leave here today changed because you know now that no act is too small and any person can leave a legacy for future generations."

When the applause died, Ezra turned his attention to Sophie. "Some of you may know Sophie Comeaux and her daughters, Amanda and Chloe. I'd like to bring them up onstage now."

What happened next was a blur. Bree rose and pulled Sophie to her feet. The girls took her hands and practically dragged her up onstage. Then somehow she stood in the glare of the spotlights with all of Latagnier watching.

Ezra knelt to envelop the girls in a hug then rose, holding one of the twins in each arm. He lifted them into the air and addressed the crowd. "Meet four of Nell Landry's success stories."

Again the applause was deafening. Sophie held tight to the podium to keep from falling over. If this man thought he was going to convince her to read the rest of that tribute, he was crazy. At this point she couldn't have spoken her name properly, much less give a speech.

"Sophie doesn't know this, but I've called her up here for more than just to give honor to Nell. You see, I was an idiot; I need to tell her that, and I don't care if the whole town hears it. I thought that what I needed was a promotion and a job in the Pentagon when what I really needed was waiting for me back here in Latagnier."

He set the girls down and rose to turn to Sophie. When his gaze collided with hers, Sophie felt the breath go out of her. She gripped the podium tighter.

"Sophie, this is going to sound crazy because I never even admitted that I love you." He turned to the audience. "I do love her, by the way. I'm just an idiot and didn't tell her."

Chloe giggled while Amanda grasped Sophie's hand.

He looked back at her. "Anyway, as I said, this is going to sound crazy, but I sat in an office in the Pentagon for three weeks with everyone calling me Lieutenant Colonel and treating me like I was a big shot. I thought it would make me happy, but it didn't. You know when I was really happy?"

She shook her head.

"Remember when we jumped on the trampoline? When we walked along the bayou? When I showed you the old schoolhouse?" He paused to smile at the girls. "Watching movies and eating popcorn with Chloe and Amanda? I could go on, but I think you get the idea."

Sophie nodded.

"Sophie, I know in my heart that God and Nell Landry put us together. I don't know why, but I do know it's a fact. Do you believe that?"

This she knew for sure. "Yes," she managed.

"I've resigned from my job to take a teaching position at the base. I'm coming home to Latagnier."

"But your promotion."

Ezra waved away her concern. "Believe it or not, they let me keep the title. I'm still a lieutenant colonel."

She smiled.

Then he dropped to one knee and took her hand. "Sophie Comeaux, I want to be the man who makes your family complete. I want to dwell with you wherever the Lord says, and I want to make Chloe and Amanda my own daughters. Will you take this orphan into your family? Will you marry me?"

thirty

Four months later

The wedding was a full-dress affair at the chapel beside
Bayou Nouvelle with Calvin and Bree as best man and maid
of honor and Chloe and Amanda as flower girls. As Sophie
waited for her cue in the dressing room off the main foyer, she
reached for the handkerchief with the picture of the Raffles
Hotel in Singapore that she'd brought from home.

Touching it to her nose, she inhaled deeply. The scent was
still there—barely. Closing her eyes, Sophie thought of Miss
Nell.

"Oh, how I wish you were here," she whispered as the sounds
of the "Wedding March" drifted beneath the closed door. She
tucked the handkerchief into her bouquet and smiled as Bree
opened the door, Chloe and Amanda a step behind her.

"Mommy, you look so pretty," Amanda said while Chloe
nodded.

"Yes, you do," Bree added with an approving nod. "You ready
to do this?"

"Yes, I'm ready," Sophie said. "Girls?"

"Ready, Mommy," they said in unison.

The girls linked arms and followed Bree down the aisle.
Sophie waited until the music rose to crescendo before stepping
out of the room.

She followed his smile and her daughters to the altar where
Ezra waited beside a nervous-looking Calvin. Before they spoke
their vows, Ezra went down on one knee and motioned for
Chloe and Amanda to join him.

"Girls," he said, "before I marry your mom, I want to ask
you something. Will you be my daughters?"

"Yes," they squealed, climbing into his arms as Sophie's heart melted with love for this amazing man.

Ezra rose, one girl cradled in the crook of each elbow. He held them that way until Calvin pulled the ring from his pocket. Placing the girls on the floor, Ezra handed each of them a small wrapped box.

Amanda looked up at Sophie. "Can we open it?"

Somehow she managed to nod while the girls tore into the lovely paper.

"Look, Mommy—it's a charm bracelet." Chloe held the silver bracelet up for Sophie to inspect. On the bracelet were three charms: a house, a cross, and a wedding cake.

"The house is to remind us we are a family," Ezra said. "The cross tells us that Jesus is our Lord, and the wedding cake. . ." He shrugged. "I guess that one's pretty obvious."

The girls donned their bracelets with the help of Ezra, then showed them off to the guests. After a moment Bree ushered the girls to their places beside her, and Ezra reached for Sophie's hand.

"Shall we make this family complete, Sophie?"

The pastor cleared his throat, and Sophie swung her attention in his direction. "I believe that's where I come in," he said. "Now, Sophie, do you take this man to be your husband?"

In short order the "I dos" were done, and she was Mrs. Ezra Landry.

&

One year later

Sophie had cut back on her hours at the hospital, and Ezra had settled into his teaching position on base. Already the general was pushing him to consider getting his qualification to teach outside the military. Ezra had even begun to pray about working toward becoming a college professor after retirement from the marines, while Sophie knew the time was drawing near to retire from nursing for a while.

Sophie had those items on her prayer list along with a few

others. Chloe and Amanda were growing out of just about everything in their closets, but she could barely find the time or energy to take them shopping. Bree had answered that prayer by taking them on an all-day shopping extravaganza that included a fitting for a set of flower-girl dresses.

Just last week the carpenters had finished the renovations, and Sophie could finally breathe clearly. The months of dust and disturbances were well worth the results, though, as the old house now boasted its original configuration again, along with a few modern updates.

The extra space had been a blessing as the girls were begging for their own rooms. Funny how now that they had the privacy they requested, they never seemed to sleep anywhere but together. One night she would find the pair curled together in Amanda's room, and the next they would be in Chloe's. It made Sophie smile to see the girls so close.

"Soph, what are you doing? We have the afternoon off. How about we enjoy it?"

"I'm just unpacking the last of the books. I'd love a walk, maybe down by Bayou Nouvelle? Just let me empty this box, okay?"

Ezra padded into the room, the one they'd set aside as his home office, and took the book from her hand. "What's this?"

Sophie smiled. "That's Nell's journal. The one she had the girls give you."

He shook it, and glitter fell on his sneakers. "Yes, it's coming back to me. Calvin made me vacuum the back of his car to get all the glitter out. He claims he's still finding it in his spare bedroom."

She leaned against his shoulder and touched the leather cover. "Did you ever read it?"

"Some of it. Never finished it, though."

"Oh, could we do that now? Look at it, I mean?"

"Sure. Come on over here, Mrs. Landry, and let's see what Granny Nell has to say." He settled on the overstuffed chair and pulled Sophie into his lap. "Are you comfortable, honey?"

Sophie kissed her husband, then maneuvered her pregnant self into a comfortable position. "I'm fine," she said. "You spoil me, you know?"

He nuzzled her cheek and kissed the tender spot on her temple. "This marine's on duty, so get used to it."

"Yes sir, Lieutenant Colonel, sir." She gave him a mock salute, then waited while he opened the journal.

"Oh, look," she said. "The story about the purple elephant really was true."

"Yes, I remember reading that. Leave it to Granny Nell to take a disaster and turn it into a great memory."

Ezra chuckled and turned the page. There, between a verse from Isaiah and a crayon drawing of stick figures, was a photograph taped to the middle of the page.

"Oh, look," Sophie said. "It's the picture of the girls and me the day I signed the adoption papers. She told me she was taking the picture as a reminder of how God had finally brought the girls home to her. I never understood what she meant by that."

"Oh?"

She snuggled closer and inhaled the soap and aftershave scent of her husband. "Yes, it was as if there was some sort of reason she wanted me to adopt the girls. Like she picked Chloe and Amanda out especially for me. I can't explain it."

Ezra lifted the photograph to reveal the writing on the back. "Honey, I think I found the explanation." Eyes glistening, Ezra removed the tape and handed her the picture. "Turn it over."

In her distinctive handwriting, Nell had written a single sentence: *"My brother Robert Boudreaux's daughters (Ezra's half sisters) with Sophie on Adoption Day."*

Ezra Landry's Better-Than-Calvin's Apple Pie

1 large egg yolk, beaten
1/4 teaspoon salt
1/2 teaspoon ground cinnamon
1/4 teaspoon ground nutmeg
3/4 cup plus 3 tablespoons all-purpose flour
5-1/2 cups peeled, sliced cooking apples
1 tablespoon lemon juice
3/4 cup sugar, separated into 1/2 cup and 1/4 cup
1/2 cup brown sugar
1/3 cup butter at room temperature
1 pie crust, unbaked

Preheat oven to 375 F. Brush bottom and sides of crust evenly with egg yolk. Bake on baking sheet about 5 minutes, until brown. Remove crust from oven. Combine sliced apples, lemon juice, 1/2 cup sugar, 1/4 cup brown sugar, 3 tablespoons flour, salt, cinnamon, and nutmeg. Mix well, then spoon into prepared crust. Mix remaining ingredients with a fork until crumbly and sprinkle over top of filling. Bake on baking sheet until topping is golden and filling is bubbling, approximately 50 minutes. Cool thoroughly, at least 4 hours, before serving. Serves 8.

A Letter To Our Readers

Dear Reader:

In order that we might better contribute to your reading enjoyment, we would appreciate your taking a few minutes to respond to the following questions. We welcome your comments and read each form and letter we receive. When completed, please return to the following:

Fiction Editor
Heartsong Presents
PO Box 719
Uhrichsville, Ohio 44683

1. Did you enjoy reading *The Dwelling Place* by Kathleen Miller?
   ❏ Very much! I would like to see more books by this author!
   ❏ Moderately. I would have enjoyed it more if

   _____

   _____

   _____

2. Are you a member of **Heartsong Presents**? ❏ Yes ❏ No
   If no, where did you purchase this book? _____

   _____

3. How would you rate, on a scale from 1 (poor) to 5 (superior), the cover design? _____

4. On a scale from 1 (poor) to 10 (superior), please rate the following elements.

   _____ Heroine   _____ Plot
   _____ Hero   _____ Inspirational theme
   _____ Setting   _____ Secondary characters

5. These characters were special because? _____
_____
_____

6. How has this book inspired your life? _____
_____
_____

7. What settings would you like to see covered in future
Heartsong Presents books? _____
_____
_____

8. What are some inspirational themes you would like to see
treated in future books? _____
_____
_____

9. Would you be interested in reading other **Heartsong Presents** titles? ☐ Yes ☐ No

10. Please check your age range:
   ☐ Under 18   ☐ 18-24
   ☐ 25-34   ☐ 35-45
   ☐ 46-55   ☐ Over 55

Name _____
Occupation _____
Address _____
City, State, Zip _____